A LIFE FOR A LIFE

ONE OF THEM HAS TO GO…

MARIA FRANKLAND

AUTONOMY
PRESS

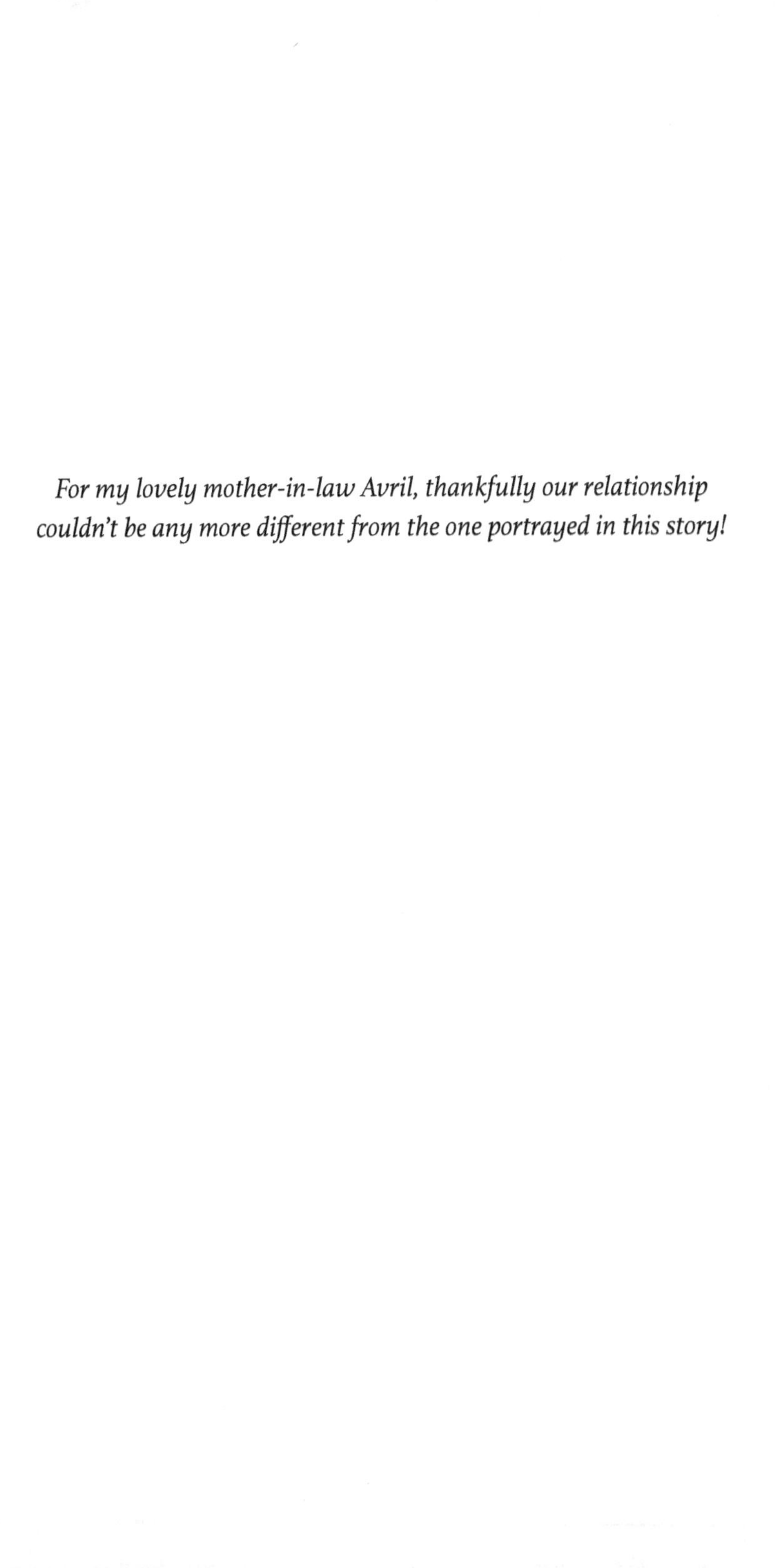

For my lovely mother-in-law Avril, thankfully our relationship couldn't be any more different from the one portrayed in this story!

JOIN MY 'KEEP IN TOUCH' LIST!

I hope you'll enjoy A Life for a Life, a story which offers a taste of my writing for you.

For another FREE psychological thriller, The Brother-in-Law, go to my website https://www.mariafrankland.co.uk to download and you'll also be added to my 'keep in touch' list.

PROLOGUE

At first, everyone at school wanted to be my friend. They all wanted to know what had happened. Chloe from next-door-but-one had seen the police cars and the ambulances, then had told the whole class.

But this week, Beth is giving out party invitations and suddenly, no one is interested in me. The horrible story at home means I am different to the rest of them. Now, I am sitting on my own in class and standing on my own in the playground. No one even wants to sit with me at lunch time. I have never been so alone.

Things aren't any better at home. I cannot remember the last time I saw Dad smile. Sometimes, I am sure I can hear him crying when I walk past his bedroom at night. I can't sleep properly anymore. When I close my eyes, I see what I saw that afternoon. I want my mum. I want my grandma. I can't see either of them anymore.

I remember when things were normal. When we got taken to our after-school activities. Ballet and horse riding for me – football and karate for my younger brother Ben. We went on holiday and sat around the table together for dinner. Me, Ben,

Mum and Dad. Ben and me don't even fight anymore. We are both too sad. I know how he feels, and he knows how I feel. It is a club no one would want to belong to.

Things changed when Granny Jeannie came to stay with us. And they will never be the same. Ever again.

1

SHAUN

My gaze switches from her glassy eyes, staring at me from the wooden floor, to the shocked eyes staring at me from the corner of my home office. "Oh my God. *Oh my God!* What the hell have you done?"

The ear-splitting bang that drew me to this room in the first place still echoes in my ears. She stands there, seemingly stunned at what she has done, as she lowers the shotgun, my shotgun, onto the desk, not taking her eyes off me the whole time. How can a life have been snuffed out so easily? Seemingly in an instant.

"That was locked in the cabinet. How did... What have you done?" I am rooted to the spot and can hardly get my words out. My gaze is drawn back to the body on the floor. And it is a body - I don't need to check if she is dead – I can see it, clear as day, without having to touch her. "What. Have. You. Done?"

Still she doesn't speak. Perhaps she's in shock. I would never, in a million years, have thought her capable of anything like this. There have always been problems, there's no denying that... I've spent years stuck in the middle of my mother and my

3

wife. My wife and my mother. It has been a nightmare. And a new one has now begun. Our lives will never be the same.

We stare at each other, the gun still too close to her. For a moment, I suspect she might use it against me too. After all, I am the only person who knows for certain what she has done. What I tell the police will decide what becomes of her. If she gets rid of me... No. Shooting me would be even more senseless than what she has already done. Killing me, I mean. After all, it was me they fought over. And the children.

We heard the bang from inside the car. Gemima and Benedict were supposed to wait there. I had told them not to move. Perhaps the boiler had exploded. That is what I had told them, whilst an icy hand of fear had clutched at my heart. Really, I knew what it was. I use that gun at least once a week for clay pigeon shooting. I know its sound as well as I know the voices of my own children.

Their heels click against the polished wooden floor and their voices echo along the hallway. They're in the doorway before I can react.

"Dad, what was that bang?"

No! They're right inside the room. Why didn't I stop them? Why didn't I lock the car? What sort of father am I?

"Dad, what's going on?"

"Benedict, Gemima, get back out there." My voice sounds alien, even to me. "Go back to the car."

They can't see this, they can't... Too late. They stand, gaping open-mouthed at the scene I have just stumbled upon. My actions feel as though they are in slow motion as I bustle them back out of the room, into the hallway, but they will never be able to unsee what they have just seen, even though only for a split second. And I know already that I can never forgive myself for putting them through this. This is the stuff of horror stories.

"What... is she...?" Gemima is gasping more than speaking. I hope she's got her asthma inhaler to hand. She is already far more mature than her nine years. She is going to have to grow up even more quickly now.

"Gemima. Take your brother to the lounge. Put the TV on. I need to call for an ambulance." My words are a gabble. I'm half in, half out of the room, keeping hold of the door. I can't believe they have glimpsed the horror beyond it. How could I have subjected them to this? "I'll be along shortly." I put my hand on the shaking shoulder of my son and try to turn him in the right direction.

Still, they both stand there, gawping at me, as though rooted to the spot, the late afternoon sunshine filtering through the window and across their innocent faces. This can't be happening. This really can't be happening.

"Go. Now!" The force of my voice surprises me. I normally never shout.

Gemima's face crumples. She breaks into a run back down the hallway, her dark hair billowing out behind her, and Benedict darts after her. I watch them run, wait until the door bangs, and return to the carnage in my office.

In the minute I have been in the hallway with Gemima and Benedict, blood has seeped across the floor and she looks even more dead than when I arrived five minutes ago. Ashen-faced and with limbs stuck out at unnatural angles – that must be how she landed. I am not sure where exactly the blood is coming from. The shooting has evidently happened at very close range, into her mouth by the looks of it which means her brain will have literally exploded inside her head. I can't look any closer. Bile is already burning at the back of my throat.

I lurch across the room to retrieve the gun. To say I'm relieved when it is given up without opposition, is an understatement. "I'm going to have to call for help," I say, as though speaking to a child. "You'll have to tell them what's happened. Why you've done what you've done."

I slide my phone from my pocket. She has got what she

wanted now, what she has *always* wanted, but there's no coming back from this.

"Ambulance please. And the police. There's been a shooting at my house. My mother and my wife. I've two children in the house. I need some help... quickly."

"I can already tell by looking at her that there won't be a pulse... yes, OK... I'll check. No. There's nothing," like I thought. "Please hurry."

I look at the figure leaning against the whitewashed wall. "What happened? Tell me."

She is wide eyed, still saying nothing, flushed in the cheeks and looking to be breathing rapidly, to the point of hyperventilation. Perhaps she can't believe what she has been capable of. It is too late for regrets.

"Well, you must tell the police what happened. There's no doubt they'll arrest you." I am stunned at my composure. If anyone could have forewarned me about this scenario, I would have imagined myself falling to pieces. But I have got to keep it together. There are the children to think of. But no sooner have I acknowledged my calm when a sudden rage engulfs me. "Why have you done this" I shout at her. "You've ruined everything. How can you just stand there, saying nothing?"

Within minutes, sirens are wailing through our suburban avenue. No doubt the neighbours will be out to speculate. It is not every day something like this happens around here. In fact, it is not any day. This street is peaceful, and joyfully uneventful. It is amazing how I am still thinking straight through all of this. I will deal with what I've got to deal with, then I will fall apart later. No doubt we will get asked to leave the house whilst they do all the forensics. I am not sure where we will go.

I throw the front door open as four armed response officers run towards the house. Before I can even start to feel relieved that I don't have to deal with things by myself anymore, that I can hand it over – lean on others, all four raise their weapons and one shouts.

"On the floor now. Hands behind your head."

"But…"

"On the floor now! Hands behind your head!" The order is even louder this time.

I kneel and place my hands on my head. My wrists are swiftly secured.

"We've received a report of a shooting," one of the armed officers says, more calmly than his colleague.

"My wife and my mother. In my office, the door at the back of the house." I can still see the horror behind it in my mind's eye. I will always see it. I jerk my head in the direction they need to go.

"Where's the weapon?"

"I've brought it out here and I've made it safe." I try to face to where it's laid on the hallway sideboard.

"Are there any other guns in the house?"

"No."

One of the other officers nods at his colleague then towards the gun. "Stay with the weapon until the forensics get here."

"Sir."

"No one must touch it. We'll need it for prints and there'll be questions to answer about its lack of safe-keeping." He turns back to me. "There's children in the house too, I understand?"

"Yes. My daughter Gemima, who's nine, and Benedict, who's seven." My soul slumps at having to admit they are in the house. If only they could have still been at school.

"Where are they?"

"Through there."

"You two search and secure the house. I'll take him to sit with his children till patrols and the DC arrives. I doubt anyone is at risk here now."

2

DANIELLE

I REMEMBER when Shaun first told me his mother was coming to stay. He didn't ask me, he *informed* me. I put up every form of resistance imaginable. I threatened to move out. To not do the housework. To stop cooking. To withhold sex. His handsome face fell with the last item on the list, but he definitely would not shift.

"If it was your mother needing some help, Danielle, there'd be no question whatsoever. If she was convalescing from a stroke, and facing going home on her own, it would be a given we'd look after her." Shaun jutted his chin out, as he always does when a subject is not up for discussion. As he gets older, he is becoming more and more stubborn. At times, I wonder if he might be going off me. Nothing works like it used to.

"But you're out at work all day Shaun. It will be *me* looking after her. She's *your* mother. This isn't fair." I had banged around our new kitchen as I ranted, taking it out on the crockery I slammed into the dishwasher. "We could at least discuss this."

"She's supposed to be your family too. You married me,

didn't you? She's your mother-in-law, for God's sake." Shaun raked his fingers through his receding fringe.

"I married *you, not* her. Not that you'd know that most of the time. It's like two for the price of one."

"It's only going to be for a few weeks Danielle."

"You're not listening, are you? I can't cope with her for a few weeks. I can't even cope with her for a few days." I slammed the dishwasher door.

"Come on love. She's not that bad. You're turning this into something it doesn't need to be." Shaun came up behind me and placed his hands on my shoulders as I gripped the edge of the sink. He obviously thought he could get around me. Not this time.

"I lived with her for eighteen years and survived to tell the tale."

"When's Granny Jeannie coming to stay?" Benedict came up behind his father and slid onto a stool at the kitchen counter. He must have been listening at the door. My children are always eavesdropping. "Can I have a drink please?" Benedict is a mini Shaun. They have exactly the same floppy, dark hair, expressive eyes and dimples. I'll be beating off the girls with big sticks when Benedict is older.

"Have you already told the children that she's coming to stay?" I looked from Benedict to Shaun who at least had the grace to look sheepish. "But I've said no!"

"Benedict, wait in the lounge, please. Your mum and I are talking. I'll bring you some juice in a minute."

We both watched as he left the kitchen, looking back at us as he went. As far as possible, we try not to have a cross word in front of the children.

"I'm going to say this once more Danielle. She's my mother." Shaun took a glass from the cupboard. "And this is my home just as much as it is yours. I have a say too. She's had a stroke, and she needs looking after."

"I don't want her here. And, as you just said, it's my home too. Don't I have a say?"

"Don't be so bloody uncharitable. I can't believe you're being like this." He poured juice into the glass, irritating me even more as he slopped it all over the counter I had just wiped down.

"If you're that bothered about your mother, go and stay in *her* flat, with her." I was saying this, but deep down, I would have been gutted if he had called my bluff.

I know my stance on the situation is going to drive a wedge between us, but I can't help it. I have spent years being compared to Jeannie. My Sunday roast, my cakes, my keeping of the house. Shaun doesn't even need to say anything sometimes – it's just the way he looks down his nose at me at something I've done, or have not done. It drives me insane, and it's getting worse.

When Jeannie is around, she takes over, or tries to. With the garden, the children, everything. She fusses, she gossips, and she treats Shaun likes he is Benedict's age. He seems to enjoy it, which infuriates me even more. And that's her behaviour in *front* of people. When she is on her so-called *best* behaviour.

When she gets me on my own, when no one else is listening, she is a different animal. She has a dig at every aspect of me. Plus, I then get compared to Saint Simone, as I call her - the woman Shaun apparently *should* have married. When I remind Jeannie that without me coming along, Gemima and Benedict would never have existed, she smiles and says, *yes but, I would never have known any different, would I?*

Once she added, *at least Simone might have given my grandchildren nice, normal names.* Jeannie insists on calling them Gem-Gem and Benny. I have given up trying to correct her. I prefer *my* parents to look after them – when Jeannie has them, they are allowed to run riot and are usually hyper for days, after being fed a diet of smarties and cola. I am sure she does it on purpose.

The row has rumbled on for days. This time, Shaun is not budging. Not one bit. This makes me just as mad as the subject we are constantly rowing about. I am not used to him not coming around to my way of thinking.

"Why won't you bloody listen," I shout at him. He is going to collect her from the hospital this morning. "I should be able to choose who comes to stay in this house, or in this case, *doesn't!*"

"And I should have a say in whether I invite my own mother who's recovering from a stroke." He glances around, presumably looking for his car keys. I should have hidden them. I'm starting to feel desperate.

"Her stroke wasn't even that bad – you know what a drama queen she is. I bet she could manage at home. We could pay for carers to go in if you're that worried."

"Carers! No chance. She needs someone with her all the time. At least for the first couple of weeks." He slides his feet into his shoes. "And how would *you* know how bad her stroke was? You haven't even bothered to visit her. Don't think that's gone unnoticed."

I ignore his comment. Wild horses wouldn't have got me to her bedside, playing the dutiful daughter-in-law. "Well, what about a convalescence home then?"

"And who would finance that Danielle?" I see something I don't like in his eyes. "Would you give up your club memberships and salon treatments?" What I see is a flicker of new-held contempt he seems to have for me. Jeannie is not even here yet and has already come between us.

I am not rising to his condescending comments either. Shaun's on a huge salary as an IT programmer and has always categorically said that he likes me being around for the kids and to manage things at home. I know I am lucky, but he doesn't need to throw it in my face.

"We can afford to pay for care for your mother for more than a week or two."

"We can certainly afford to bring her into our home for a couple of weeks and take care of her ourselves. Anyway, it's sorted now, it's all in her discharge plan. I'm about to go and collect her."

"But it will be *me* looking after her, not you!"

"Actually, I've booked time off work – until she starts physio. A-ha." His hand lands on his car keys on the windowsill.

"So why haven't you mentioned this before? You need to keep your time off." Fury washes over me. "So because your mother comes to stay, we have to do without one of our family holidays. It just gets better and better. I live for our holidays Shaun. When it's just us and the children. Which is how our home should be as well."

"It's only for two weeks. Danielle, I'm fed up of repeating this to you. Then life will go back to normal."

"It won't be a couple of weeks though, will it? Once that woman's here, we'll never be able to get rid of her."

"*That woman* is my mother. I'm sick of it Danielle. Your mother does my head in sometimes, but I keep my negative thoughts to myself. You make her welcome when we get back, or else, go and stay with your parents or something. I mean it."

"So you're issuing threats now," I shout after him as he ducks under the kitchen doorway. "We need to sort this out Shaun." She has really got in between us.

The slam of the door echoes through the house. The next time I see him, he'll have *her* with him. I wrestle with the urge to do as he suggests and pack some things for me and the children. But why should I be the one who clears off?

3

JEANNIE

I'M happy to allow them all to think I'm sicker than I am. The truth is, I'm as tough as old boots, and the hospital physio has been delighted with my progress. Today I had to make a cup of tea. True, I was a bit shaky, probably because I haven't been out of bed for over a week, but I managed it easily enough. Then I had to show that I could get dressed on my own and manage a flight of stairs by myself. Apart from still being slightly weak down one side, this was fine.

Obviously, I've made out that this weakness is worse than it really is. I would definitely be able to manage at home, but I would rather be discharged to my son's house. No matter how much I see of him, it's never enough. And of course, it's lovely to spend time with Gem-Gem and Benny. It's such a shame about Danielle, my daughter-in-law. This stay of mine is make or break.

∾

"We'd like you to stay with us, when you get discharged Mum." Shaun had pulled a chair up to my bedside. It always gave me a lift when he walked onto the ward. The other ladies liked him too and made him blush by telling him how handsome he is.

"*We?*" I thought I was hearing things. Surely Danielle isn't in agreement?

"Yes. I've run it by Danielle and she's OK about it." He reached for my hand. He's definitely become more affectionate. I guess nobody really knows how much someone means to them until a life-threatening illness comes to call.

"Just OK?" I should have been happy with that, really. If Shaun had said Danielle was *delighted* about it, I would have probably fallen out of bed in shock.

"Honestly Mum. We don't want you going back to your flat. Not yet. We want to look after you. It's about time you had someone looking after you. You've taken care of us enough over the years."

"Ah, but you know that's my favourite thing to do, don't you?"

He is such a good boy is Shaun, and has never been any trouble. I'm so proud of how well he has done for himself and those two beautiful grandchildren he's given me. I love being around young ones again. But I bet Danielle will let me have them even less after this wretched stroke. She will say I'm not fit, or similar. Anything to come between us as much as she can. Just because she disagrees with my little nicknames for them, and the treats I give them.

I'll always remember the first time Shaun brought Danielle home to meet me. I was under strict instructions from Bob not to mention Simone, the break-up, or my misgivings about Shaun's new relationship. I'd been ordered, and I mean *ordered,* to give Danielle a chance. As we sat around the table, the hairs literally stood up on the back of my neck. I couldn't put my finger on it, but I knew she was trouble and I'm a very good judge of character. When something's off, it's off. Shaun was convinced he was punching above his weight, and spent six months grinning from ear to ear. I really tried to be happy for him.

There's no denying it, with her model-like figure, even after two kids, and her long, blonde glossy hair, I can see why he was, and still is, attracted to her. And that's maybe why she's always had so much control over him. Where they go. What they do. Where they live. Who they spend their time with. Not me usually, when she has her way. Even her parents are wrapped around her manicured little finger. What Danielle wants, Danielle gets. She always has.

In the run up to the stroke, I saw Shaun less and less frequently, despite them only living in the next town. I went to pieces when Bob died two years ago, and Shaun was around to check on me quite a lot then. But before long, the visits and the calls petered out. I guessed Danielle was behind it – she normally is. When he was here, she would ring to see where he was, and when he would be back. Anyone would have thought she'd have been glad of the peace, as nine times out of ten, Shaun had the children with him. I lived for their visits, especially after losing Bob.

A look would cross his face when he saw it was *her* on the phone. One that I used to see when he was accused of something as a boy. He'd move away from us to speak to her, probably not wanting me to hear anything of their conversation. I'd have loved to give her a piece of my mind. Fancy giving him a hard time for visiting his own mother. I bet Shaun never tried coming between Danielle and her parents.

∼

I'm glad to be getting discharged from hospital today, despite having made some friends in here. I've even taken a few of their phone numbers. It's been ten days since they brought me in, and I've been well looked after, but now crave to experience the sunshine and blue sky visible beyond the window of the ward.

Shaun has a gorgeous garden I might be able to sit in, if the days are still as mild as they were before being admitted to hospital. I'm very relieved not to be returning to the flat just yet. That horrible day when this happened would come flooding back to me.

I'd had the most unimaginable pain in one side of my head, and the vision in one eye had gone since I'd got up that morning. I also felt as sick as a dog. At first, I thought it was a migraine, took some tablets and laid on the sofa to give them a chance to work. But when I developed numbness down one side, and my thinking became foggy and muddled, I knew there was a chance I was having a stroke.

I'd managed to attract the attention of Margaret in the flat opposite by banging on the window. Thankfully my front door was unlocked, as by the time she got to me, I was slipping into unconsciousness. I have a vague memory of her telling me to smile and wondering what on earth there was to smile about. Then she was trying to get me to raise my arms above my head. Clearly, she had watched all the stroke public information films.

"What's your name?" she'd asked.

She knows exactly what my name is, I'd thought at the time. Then I realised I couldn't speak. I knew what words I was trying to formulate but must have been completely incoherent. I heard the panic in Margaret's voice when she made the phone call. My neighbour... having a stroke... conscious but drowsy... Jeannie Harrington.

The next thing I knew, I was waking in hospital, groggy and thirstier than I've ever been. I'd lost three days and had an exhaustion like I'd never felt before.

"Nurse. Nurse!" Shaun had jumped up and two people rushed in. He looked crumpled and unkempt. Clearly, he had been keeping a vigil. My heart melted at the thought of my son waiting at the side of me, willing me to get better.

Since then, I've battled to get well. But they want my bed. Of course they want my bed. I could go to a nursing home, convalescence home, my own home, with help, or somewhere else. It delighted me when Shaun suggested I stay with them. I can't wait to have more time with my grandchildren. Me and Danielle being forced together may do us some good – I'll see when I get there. Perhaps it is time to put us to the test. Yet, I still don't know how he's talked her into it.

~

"It's home time Mum." I open one eye to see Shaun looking over me.

"I'm sorry. I was awake really early this morning. Someone in the next bed was snoring."

"You don't have to apologise Mum. You're allowed to have a sleep. It'll do you good. You can rest as much as you need to when you get to ours. You've got your own en-suite room and everything. Danielle's made it nice for you."

I wonder what *and* everything means. Probably Danielle's hostility, but Shaun will be blind to that and will only see what she wants him to see. I haul myself up to look at him. I'm drowsy like this a lot. At times, I can hardly keep my eyes open. I feel very old at the moment.

"You always used to tell me that sleep was the best medicine when I was growing up Mum."

Those were my favourite days. When we were a family. Me, Bob and Shaun. I'd wanted more children, but it never happened. I would have loved a daughter. When Shaun was with the girlfriend he had before Danielle, Simone, she became almost like a daughter to me. They were engaged to marry, then Shaun was unfaithful with Danielle. I've never been so upset in my life. I begged and pleaded with Shaun to do the right thing, but he said he was in love with Danielle.

Goodness knows what he saw in her, apart from the obvious physicality. No one knows I'm still in touch with Simone. We meet regularly for coffee. She's married now so there's no chance of me being able to engineer some sort of reconciliation between her and Shaun. I would if I could. And they've all got children now, but who knows what could happen in the future?

"When can we go then?" My speech sounds strange as one side of my face is still numb. It's coming back slowly. I hope the children will get used to me sounding different.

"You need a final check over and your meds Mum. The children can't wait to see their Granny Jeannie."

"I can't wait to see them too. And to eat something other than hospital food." I try to swing my legs over the side of the bed. Every time I try to do something, I'm always surprised by the level of weakness this wretched stroke has left with me - I will beat it though. I will get back to as much normal as I can. "What about Danielle?"

"What about her?"

"Are you sure she's...?"

"Sssh Mum. She's even put flowers in your room. She's glad to help - honestly."

I find that hard to believe, but bite my lip against a reply. People can change. Even Danielle. Maybe I should try to give her the benefit of the doubt. I can hardly believe she's put flowers in my room. Maybe she's had a personality transplant.

4

DANIELLE

I PACE up and down in front of the bay window, surprised to notice my fists bunched at my sides. I spoke to Dad on the phone earlier and put him on standby, alerting him I might turn up with the children if it gets too much here. He wasn't as sympathetic as Mum had been when I spoke to her.

He said, "Oh Danielle, Jeannie's not that bad. I bet she's really grateful that you're both welcoming her into your home whilst she gets better." I reckon he said that because he'll be thinking about what happens to him if he gets ill in the future.

Any minute now, this house, my home, will be invaded. Life, as I know it, is about to change beyond recognition. To make matters worse, Gemima and Benedict are actually excited that Granny Jeannie is going to be here when they get home from school. I feel like they're betraying me.

If I got on with my mother-in-law, this wouldn't be such a disposition. And what Shaun doesn't understand about me, is that I need to be part of any decision making process. Especially when it directly affects me. He didn't even ask me if I was OK with having Jeannie come to stay with us – he told me.

It's like I don't have any power or control over my own life, or who comes to stay in my home.

If it were one of my parents that was ill, they simply wouldn't impose in this way. I have a feeling that once she's here, we'll never get rid of her. I haven't been to visit her whilst she has been in hospital, so don't really know what to expect when she gets here. I couldn't bring myself to play the part of the concerned daughter-in-law, when deep down, I cannot stand her. And this is her own fault.

I throw myself into my armchair, the depth of my sigh taking me aback. I close my eyes. I'm going to have to try with her. I'm going to have to. Moments later, I hear the throaty engine of Shaun's Land Rover. Here we bloody go. Fury rises in me like a serpent.

I should go out and help her in, welcome her, but I cannot bring myself to. I watch from the other side of the lounge, hoping neither of them will see me from the outside. Shaun gets out first, rising to his six foot two height as he strides around the car to open the door for his mother. He seems to be in a better mood than the one he left in.

Jeannie looks frailer than I imagined, and I'm shocked to see her steadying herself with a stick. Although, harsh as it sounds, I'm really not convinced that it isn't all an act. She's been clinging to Shaun since Bob died. She's only just into her seventies, but I know that strokes run in their family. Shaun, although only in his mid-thirties, is careful about his own diet and lifestyle. It was a stroke that killed his father and his maternal grandfather.

Jeannie hooks her arm into Shaun's and they make their way towards the porch. This mother and son unity annoys me. It always has. I think it boils down to the fear that Shaun is more devoted to her than to me, Gemima and Benedict. All his mother ever has to do is click her fingers, and he goes running. Not that she sees it like that. She's always complaining that she doesn't see enough of him. Or our kids. And of course she blames me for this. She's said so several times, however she usually saves her nastiest comments for when she knows Shaun isn't listening. That's one thing I hate about her the most – her deviousness. Then making out like it's all me.

"Danielle. Are you in? We're back." Gosh, he sounds positively friendly.

The front door bangs against the side wall, which irritates me further. *How many times have I told him about that?*

"Danielle! We'll get you sat down in a minute Mum."

I face them both in the hallway, looking from Jeannie's watery eyes to Shaun's quiet brown ones. There's no denying Shaun looks like his mother in the face, but he's tall and stocky like his father was. She wasn't as bad when Bob was still alive. He was alright, was Bob, and he would stick up for me in front of Jeannie, but she's got much worse with me since he died. He kept her in check to a certain extent, and had a look that would put Jeannie in her place. That was another bone of contention for her. She hated that I got on with her husband. Once, when no one was in earshot, she accused me of having designs on him! That was hilarious.

Shaun helps Jeannie lower herself into the chair in the corner of the hallway. To be fair, she looks like she cannot go another step, and I do wonder, for a moment, whether she could have managed on her own in her flat after all.

"Hello Danielle." Her voice is stiff, and she won't look at me.

"Jeannie."

"How are you?" she asks. It's typical of her to come out of hospital and fire a wellbeing question at me first.

"Good, thank you. Yourself?"

"I've been better, to be fair."

Her voice is strange, the words slurred like she's had a drink. I should feel sorry for her, but I'm struggling to muster any sympathy. I can't ever imagine us getting beyond how we feel about each other, though I've often hoped we might. I'm so envious of the friends I have who get on with their mothers-in-law.

"I'll put the kettle on." Shaun hangs Jeannie's coat up. "I bet you're ready for a decent cuppa Mum, after that watery stuff at the hospital."

"I'll do it," I blurt. I'm not being left on my own with her to make small talk. I can't think of anything worse.

Perhaps it wouldn't have been so bad if he wasn't an only child – we might have been able to share this burden with someone else. Obviously, if she'd been half civil to me, in the time I've known her, I wouldn't see her as a burden – I would be glad to help.

Shaun raises an eyebrow as I return, my tray laden with three mugs. I've relented and put some biscuits on a plate. It will be interesting to see whether she can eat. No doubt, she'll exaggerate the after-effects of the stroke and will milk it for as long as possible.

"Come on Mum." He picks up the walking stick from beside her. "Let's get you into the lounge. It's warmer and comfier in there. We've lit the fire."

"Oooh lovely. I do like a proper fire. I'm so pleased you're off work for a couple of weeks Shaun." She smiles a lopsided smile as she gets back to her feet, supported by him.

"Wouldn't you be more comfortable in your room Jeannie?" I use the sweetest voice I can muster, but Shaun sees right through me.

"No Danielle." His expression flashes a warning look at me. "She wouldn't."

She makes a right song and dance of transporting herself from the hallway chair to the armchair in the lounge. Eventually the puffing and panting subsides, and I pass her a mug of tea. Shaun immediately intervenes.

"Everything needs to be passed to her good side, to start

with," he says, frowning at me. "Are you alright with drinking that on your own Mum, or do you need some help?"

God. The whole situation is making me want to scream. Maybe I *should* stay at Mum and Dad's like he suggested. But I'd want Gemima and Benedict with me, and Shaun wouldn't stand for that – I don't think he would let me take them.

"I'll manage thanks Shaun. I need to get used to doing things myself. I don't want to outstay my welcome here." She raises the mug to the right-hand side of her mouth and slurps. Tea dribbles down her chin. I watch as she chews on a biscuit and it's almost too much for me, watching chewed up biscuit mixed with tea dribbling from her chin onto her cardigan. She looks at me from the corner of her eye.

At least I've got my physio friend, Leanne, lined up to assess her in a couple of days. She'll provide me with an honest opinion, and get Jeannie on her feet faster than the weekly NHS physio would. They're not even sending anybody until next week.

Shaun wipes his mother's mouth. I never thought I would see the day. "Shouldn't you be picking the kids up love?"

At least he's calling me love. There has not been a great deal of affection between us this last week. We've been too busy rowing.

"I'm setting off after I've drunk this." I grimace inwardly as Jeannie slurps again. How the hell am I going to cope? Two weeks of *this*? No chance.

"I'm so tired." Jeannie looks at Shaun. "I can hardly keep my eyes open. I wish I could get my energy levels back to normal."

"I've made up the spare room," I say, something lifting inside me. Once she's up there, it will be easier to keep her up there. I will almost be able to pretend she's not here at all. Looking at the state of her, or at least the state she is presenting to us, she'd be better off convalescing in bed, anyway. "I've put a nice bunch of flowers in there to cheer you up."

5

JEANNIE

"I don't want to eat my dinner in bed." I raise myself onto my elbows to look at my daughter-in-law framed in the doorway, the landing light behind her, holding a tray. I can't believe it's dark already. Part of me feels as though I've been sleeping for hours, yet another part of me feels as though I've only just closed my eyes. "I want to see the children." Now it's dark, I feel low. Spending time with Gem-Gem and Benny will sort me out.

"Now come on Jeannie. We both know you're better off in here for now." Danielle snaps the main light on and walks towards my bed. She places the tray on the over-bed table, which she slides towards me. I stare at mash, vegetables and chicken breast, cut into small pieces like I'm five years old.

"Shaun's even cut it up for you." She smiles, but it's one that doesn't meet her eyes. "How roles have reversed between you."

Snarky cow. But right now she can make the difference between me slipping deeper into a depressed state or helping me to lift myself out of it.

"Please Danielle. I don't want to be up here on my own all night." I can't believe I'm pleading with her to allow me to go downstairs. "The walls will close in on me up here."

"I've made your room nice for you Jeannie. You could show a bit more gratitude. Anyway, you'll be home as soon as is possible." Her eyes are stone cold as usual. Shaun said she was OK about me coming. I think Shaun was lying.

"Can you get those flowers out of here, please? They're making me feel ill." She knows full well that lilies give me migraines. I'm certain that's why she put them in here.

I watch as she marches over to the dressing table and yanks the vase from it.

"You didn't want me here in the first place, did you?"

"No, I didn't." She swings around to look at me. "But we'll have to make the best of it, won't we? It's what Shaun wants." She stands with one hand on her hip, her lip curling with dislike towards me.

"Shoving me up here, out of the way, is hardly *making the best of it*?" Tears fill my eyes. I was looking forward to being around Shaun and the kids. I've felt so down since my stroke. The thought of getting here and being with family was keeping me going. I say nothing about this because I can't include Danielle in the people I was looking forward to spending time with, and besides, she will jump on any sign of weakness in me. "Can you send Shaun up please? Now? I want a word with him."

"He's eating his dinner. I'll ask him to come up later."

"Later? I don't want to be on my own until later. Shaun!" I call out, but my voice feels and sounds strangely feeble. "I bet you wish I'd died, don't you?" There, I've said it. She didn't bother to visit me in hospital. Yet, I would bet she would not have stood in the way of Shaun's inheritance if I had. Hypocrite. I have a mind to leave everything I've got straight to the kids so she can't get her hands on a penny. She's had enough handed to her on a plate as it is.

"Your son has made it perfectly clear that it doesn't matter what I want or don't want." She puts the vase down, and her skirt swishes around her legs as she walks to the window and yanks the curtains together. "Eat your dinner Jeannie, before it gets cold." Then in a sarcastic tone, she adds, "You need to get your strength back. Quickly."

"You've probably laced it with something."

"I don't have to put up with this. I'm off for my dinner with my family. I'll leave you to it." She strides back towards the door, her bracelets rattling as she goes.

"Take those flowers with you."

Bitch. Her footsteps die away, and I can just about hear the faraway voices of Gem-Gem and Benny. I wonder if they even know I'm up here – it seems unusual that they haven't been to see me. Surely Shaun will have told them that I've arrived.

I stab my fork into a piece of chicken and try to chew. My arm still feels a bit weak. I can only chew properly at one side too. The mashed potatoes are easier to manage. But I'm not hungry. How can a person eat when they're trying not to cry? I toss the fork back onto the plate, splashing the spotless white eiderdown with gravy. I can't believe she's making me eat alone in bed. I'm not having it. She can't treat me like this. I push the table away with my foot.

Normally I would be able to rescue the calamity that follows but I can't move very quickly at the moment. All goes into slow motion as the table falls to the floor with a crash, splattering gravy all over the pristine oatmeal carpet and up the magnolia wall.

I stare in shock at the mess I have created for a moment, then listen as several sets of footsteps rumble up the staircase.

"Mum!" Shaun is first to appear in the doorway, closely followed by the children. "Are you OK? What was that crash?"

"I – it was an accident."

Shaun looks from me to the floor. "How on earth..."

"Uh-oh. Mum's going to go mad when she sees this." Gem-Gem walks into the room and steps over the gravy. It's lovely to see the little face that appears at my bedside. It feels like ages since I last saw it. The dear face of Benedict appears beside it.

"What the…" Danielle strides towards the mess and stands, hands on hips glaring at me. "You've done this on purpose, haven't you Jeannie?"

"It was an accident Mum." Gemima gapes at her, open-mouthed.

"Of course I haven't. I was trying to move the table with my foot, and…"

"Just because you didn't want to eat upstairs," Danielle snaps.

"I wanted to spend time with my family. Not eat alone in bed." I reach with my good hand for Gemima's hand, which she grips. "Why haven't you even let the children come up to say hello yet?"

"You were sleeping Mum." Shaun sets about scraping the food from the carpet. "They were going to come and see you when they'd eaten."

"I wouldn't bother." Danielle's nostrils flare, and her face is furious and pinched. "Thanks to your mother, the carpet's ruined. God, she's not even been here for a day."

"Is it heck. We'll get the carpet cleaner on it. It will be as good as new."

"*You'll* get the carpet cleaner on it Shaun. She's your mother. I'm going to eat my dinner. Benedict. Gemima – downstairs, now please."

"But Mum. I want to see Grandma." Benny sidles around the side of his sister. "Can she have some more dinner? Can I eat my dinner up here with her?"

"No," Danielle says. "Get downstairs."

At her raised voice, the children both scuttle towards the door.

"Why does she have to be like this?" I try to sit up some more so I can see Shaun's face. From where I am, I can only see the spike of his hair. I'm surprised he did not stick up for me more. Probably because of the hard time she'll give him if he does. I thought he was developing more backbone recently.

"We've not had the carpet long, that's all. You know what she's like about the house – it's her pride and joy." He raises himself higher on his knees, so he's level with the bed. "Take no notice Mum – she doesn't mean any harm. She'll be back up here before long to say she's sorry, I'm sure."

"Like hell. She doesn't want me here. You know that as well as I do."

"Mum. I'm sorry to have to ask this, but you didn't make this mess on purpose, did you? If I don't ask you, she'll only have a go at me."

"I can't believe you need to ask me that." Tears stab at my eyes. Maybe I should have gone home, after all. "Of course I didn't Shaun. It was an accident. I was moving the table away with my foot."

"I'll bring you some more dinner Mum. And I'll sit and eat mine with you." He rises from the floor. "Then when we've eaten, me and the kids will sit with you and have a game. How about Ludo?"

I smile at him then, everything within me lighting up. "Only if you promise not to take advantage of me being under par." Danielle's miserable little plan to ostracise me has backfired. She's only succeeded in ostracising *herself*. Maybe whilst I'm here – I can help Shaun develop that backbone of his.

6

DANIELLE

I FASTEN the children's lunchboxes and sit them on top of their respective bookbags. "Right you two, coats and shoes on please." I'll be glad to get out of this house. Especially after spending most of last night sat on my own whilst they all played happy families. Thank God I had wine in the house.

"Can we go and see Grandma to say goodbye?" Benedict looks up from his cereal bowl.

"Pleeeeeese." Gemima chimes in.

"No, you can't. We'll be late." I'm snapping at them, but I don't care. "You can see her later."

Although I've told no one that I've already planned to take the children shopping when I pick them up later. Then we might go for tea somewhere. The only way I can cope with Jeannie staying in my house against my wishes, is to get out of the way. I'm not having a repeat of last night. I left Jeannie in her room to get out of the way, not imagining that my family would spend the evening sat up there with her. Perhaps if Shaun misses me and the children for a while, along with other things that I won't be doing with him, or for him, he'll see sense and make other arrangements for his spoilt bloody mother.

Hopefully, he'll wonder where I am when I don't come back. This ploy always used to work with him.

"Of course the kids can say goodbye to their grandma." Shaun strides into the kitchen. "Go on kids, just don't be long. And don't climb onto the bed. Grandma is still getting better."

I wasn't aware he was listening. They both dash to the door, pushing each other out of the way to get to their bloody grandmother.

"You had no right saying yes to them when I've just said no." I toss a knife into the dishwasher. "We've discussed this before. We shouldn't be undermining each other in front of the children. Is your mother even awake yet? You were up there late enough last night. It's a wonder the children managed to get up this morning."

"You know as well as I do that she's awake." Shaun has changed so much since his mother arrived. "You must have heard me talking to her whilst you were getting ready." There has been a distance since he chose to overrule me and invite her here. The gulf between us seems to be widening by the hour. "You need to get a grip Danielle. You've been a nightmare recently."

"I've been a nightmare! You try having someone forced on you. That's what I've had to put up with."

"She's my bloody mother. Of course I want to look after her whilst she's ill. We'd do the same for yours, wouldn't we?"

"That argument's wearing thin now. Anyway, Jeannie's starting physio today. We'll have her back on her feet within a couple of weeks, I reckon."

"What do you mean, Mum's starting physio?" He turns and looks at me, frowning. "*Says who?* I thought the hospital said we were waiting at least two weeks. To get her rested and strong enough for physio first."

"Leanne will be here at eleven. She's going to come every other day. I've told her to bill your mother directly."

"You've arranged this without even discussing it with me? Or my mum for that matter?"

"Do you want your mother to get better or don't you? She's more than strong enough to start." To prove my point, I can hear the kids shrieking and laughing from the room above us which irritates me beyond measure. She lays there, pretending to be ill, yet she can lark around with my children. "The NHS physio was only planning to come once a week. That's neither here nor there. Leanne has fit her in as a special favour. She's very good."

I don't tell him that Leanne has raised her fee to make appointments at such short notice, and to travel outside her normal area. I've been friends with her for years and know she will be honest with me about Jeannie's progress, and won't put up with any nonsense from her either. Leanne is my best chance of getting Jeannie home as quickly as possible so we can get back to normal.

"I don't care how *good she is.* You should *not* be making decisions like that without consulting me first. She's *my* mother."

"You've room to talk about decision making. I never wanted her here."

"Why are you shouting Mum?" Two anxious faces appear in the kitchen doorway looking from me to their dad. We never normally shout, and to be honest, I didn't realise we were.

"If the children heard us, Mum will have too." Shaun slams breakfast bowls into the dishwasher. "You need to sort yourself out Danielle. She's trying to get herself better and doesn't need extra stress."

"Get your stuff, you two." Blinkered by tears, I stagger towards the kitchen door. I just want to get out of here. "Like I said, Leanne will be here at eleven."

"Where are you going? Won't you be back when she comes?"

"Anywhere but here. Well done Shaun. You and your mother have managed to drive me out of my own house." At least he's accepted the fact that Leanne is coming.

"You're driving yourself out. You're being stupid. Why can't you just get along with her?"

"Grandma's going to play another game with us when we get home," Gemima says as we turn the final corner and approach the school gates.

You want to bet? I feel like saying.

"I enjoy having her to stay at our house," adds Benedict. "Don't you Mummy?" He gives me a look like his father would give me.

The way I'm feeling, his words are a knife through my chest. Rightly or wrongly, I feel like my own children should be on my side. "Of course."

I pull the Land Rover up at the side of the kerb, ignoring the hard stares I'm getting from some of the other mothers. One of them points at the *no parking* sign above her. If they were not so utterly unfriendly, I might want to get out of my vehicle from time to time. I feel as lonely amongst these women as I do in my own home. The children have only been here for a couple of years. They've made loads of friends whereas I have not made a single one.

I swing the Land Rover around in the school entrance, the throaty acceleration eliciting more hostile looks. I'm unpopular here, I'm unpopular at home and I'm utterly fed up. Jeannie might be meek and mild at the moment whilst she is supposedly ill, but she'll be back to her usual nasty self any time. The self that has sly digs at me at every opportunity and makes me feel like an outsider in my own family.

I pull up at the park. A walk might straighten my jumbled

thinking out. I trudge along, my feet tapping against the tarmac as I pull my coat tighter around myself. It's one of those drizzly days that is making me feel even more dreary.

I don't know what's happened to Shaun. I used to be able to twist him around my little finger as much as I can my parents, but just lately, he's changed. And I think there's more to it than merely his mother's illness. I miss him.

"A shopping trip sounds like what you need Danielle." It's wonderful to hear Mum's friendly voice over the phone as I sink onto a bench. I haven't seen her for a fortnight as they've been away and only got back at the weekend. They could not have timed their return any better. "How about I meet you at the Pavilion Centre in half an hour? We'll start with a coffee and then I'll treat you to that handbag you've had your eye on. I've brought you all a present back from Cape Verde as well."

I brighten at the thought of not having to go home, to the chilly atmosphere and Jeannie's demands. At least I no longer have to feel as though I have time to kill – not now I'm meeting Mum. I usually love it when Shaun takes a holiday from work, but on this occasion, we're not getting any time together. His impromptu leave now means two weeks less of availability for us to go away as a family. That was one of my arguments when he mentioned his mother coming to stay with us. Well, I'll show him. Whilst he's having to work, I'll take Gemima and Benedict away with Mum and Dad. It will be great. They'll help me with the children – I'll be able to read, shop, sunbathe...

My parents are amazing, especially Mum. There's never been a time when they've not been there for me. Being an only child, I know I've been spoiled rotten. At one time, Mum was told she would struggle to conceive - she had some hormone problem or other, so when I came along, they were over the moon. Gemima and Benedict have been the icing on the cake for them, and Dad was crying when I told him I was having a boy. As much as he loves me, I was never interested in trains or fishing, not like Benedict is. They've got a wonderful bond.

My parents have never been short of money and if I ever wanted something, I got it. The other girls at school were jealous of me as we were growing up. I was the first to have the latest bike, stereo, or whatever – as well as the best clothes – I suppose I took it for granted. Shaun had to promise Mum that he'd look after me in the same way when we got married.

She will not be happy when she hears what is going on, and how I've been side lined for Jeannie.

7

JEANNIE

"Grip my hand as tightly as your can." I like Leanne, my new physiotherapist. And I'm a very good judge of character. I've been proven right with Danielle, haven't I? Shaun dotes on her and if it were reciprocated, I wouldn't be so judgmental. But the poor man even has to iron his own clothes. And it's not as if she works. She even has a cleaner for the house and gets the food shop delivered.

Women nowadays do not know how good they've got it. I'm not sure what she actually does with her time, other than spend the money my son single-handedly works so hard for, on herself, normally.

I can't believe someone as nice as Leanne is even friends with Danielle. I was very annoyed to begin with that a private physio had been hired, especially when I discovered she's friends with Danielle. I'm going to be seeing an NHS one every week, but this one is scheduled to come every other day. That's how desperate Danielle is to get me back home. She's told Leanne to bill me directly, but Shaun has already stepped in there. So that's backfired on her too. She underestimates my son, clearly.

"OK, can you swing your legs out of bed?" I do as Leanne asks. I've been practicing this. She's already remarked that I'm further forwards than she would have expected at this stage. I should probably hold back a bit and not make too much progress – I don't want Danielle packing me off home. The thought of being on my own fills me with a renewed depression.

"Get your feet flat on the floor. Good stuff. Well done." Leanne's a pretty girl with a warmth in her face that Danielle has never had. I heard her and Shaun going at each other this morning. If circumstances were different, I would be sorry to come between them, but if I highlight the cracks between them now, then maybe that isn't such a bad thing. I've so often fantasised about Shaun and Danielle splitting up.

Maybe Shaun would have to come and live in the flat with me for a while – lots of men have to stay with their parents when a marriage breaks up. It would be wonderful to have him around, and of course, that would mean I would have the children come to stay at weekends.

Or maybe, if it gets bad enough, and not wanting to uproot the children, Danielle would leave them here with Shaun, and move in with her parents. Shaun is probably more hands on with them than she is, so maybe she would leave them with him. Of course, I could stay here permanently to help. This room is nice enough. I could definitely cope with staying here. And I've always wanted an en-suite.

"Right Jeannie. Let's see how you are with the stairs next, shall we?"

"The physio in the hospital had me going up and down stairs before they discharged me. I had a stick to help though."

"And what about since you got here?"

"No. I just came up them the once."

"The once? But this is your third day since you were discharged. Have you not been downstairs at all?"

"No. Danielle doesn't want me down there. She wants me up here, well out of her way."

"Aww, I'm sure that's not the case." Leanne frowns as she looks up at me from where she is kneeling on the floor. Her hair is piled into a knot on the top of her head. From the angle I'm watching her from, she's the spitting image of Simone, Shaun's ex. I wonder if he noticed this when he let her in. He must have done. She has the same slim and willowy build. And she's pretty without any effort. There's no make-up, nail varnish or jewellery. Unlike Danielle who's always done up like a dog's dinner.

"It's true. I've heard it from the horse's mouth. She even makes me eat my meals up here. It's why she's hired you – to get me back on my feet and get me home quicker." I'm on a roll now. "She nearly fell out with Shaun over his insistence that I come here. I've really come between them."

She rises from the floor and picks up her bag. "Danielle sounded really concerned about you when we spoke on the phone last week. She wanted me to help you."

"That's because she wants me home as quickly as possible, and not here."

Leanne shakes her head, her bun wobbling with the movement. "Jeannie, I'm not sure if you know, but Danielle and I are friends. That's the only reason I was able to fit you in so quickly – as a favour. She's honestly *never* said anything untoward about you, not to me anyway, and I think…"

"Trust me Leanne. If this house was on fire, she would leave me to burn in it. They were her exact words to me yesterday. She only ever says things like that when no one else is around. You only see and hear what Danielle wants you to see and hear. It's all a front. You don't know her like I do."

Her eyes widen, but she says nothing. But I know she'll have to log what I've said though. She'll probably even have to report it. In my current state, it will undoubtedly be a safeguarding issue. It's verbal, psychological, and emotional abuse. Even I know that.

It's probably time to change the subject, although I'm going to keep chipping away. In the meantime, I need to get Leanne and Shaun into each other's company. "Are you friends with my son as well as Leanne?"

"Today is the first time I've met him. He seems very nice though. Shuffle to the edge of the bed and hold onto me." She stretches her arm out. "Let's get you up."

"Are you married?" I realise I'm maybe being too forward asking that, especially on the back of mentioning Shaun. I get slowly to my feet.

She smiles a smile which lights up her whole face. "No, I'm single... but I'm happily single. It would take someone really special for me to give up my freedom. Besides, my work keeps me busy."

I warm to her even more. She's so different from Danielle, who probably waited her whole life for someone like Shaun to come along. Leanne has got her own life and profession. I'm not sure Danielle has ever worked. From what I can tell, she messed about doing nails for people before her and Shaun got married, and then used the children as an excuse for not returning afterwards, claiming that she was going to be a stay at home mum. I blame Shaun as much as her. He should never have allowed it. I've never not worked. Women should contribute to the household as much as men.

"I'm so glad to be going downstairs?" I say. "I'm climbing the walls stuck up here." I want to be down there when Danielle returns. That will really get her back up. "Maybe I could make you a cup of tea Leanne. That was something else I had to do before I could leave the hospital."

"It sounds like a plan. Right, let's see how you are with your walking. Keep your arm linked with mine as we go."

It's good to feel a connection with another human being.

Shaun has never been the most affectionate creature on the planet, again, like his dad, and Danielle has hardly even been allowing the children to come up and see me. Usually I can count on plenty of hugs from them.

I'm used to getting out of bed to shuffle to the loo. But it feels strange as I begin to descend the stairs, my slippers sinking into the thick carpet.

"You're doing great Jeannie."

At least if I end up having to go home, in my flat I don't have stairs to contend with. But they're a small price to pay if I can stay here. Especially if I can get Danielle out of the way. For good. "Do you think so?" I tug her arm closer to me. "It's because I've got such a good physio."

Shaun appears at the bottom. "Is she OK to be coming up and down stairs? Danielle thought it might be safer if she didn't."

"I'd say so. In fact, she seems to be getting bored and lonely in her room, aren't you Jeannie? A change of scenery will do her good."

I nod, resisting the urge to say, *well said.* But I'm pretending to channel my effort and attention into safely putting one foot in front of the other. If I don't talk much, Leanne and Shaun will feel encouraged to talk to each other. I can't believe how weak I have ended up down my left-hand side, which is what I would normally use to hold onto the bannister. I feel fine having Leanne supporting me on the right though. If someone is with me, it will give me more confidence to be going up and down them a bit quicker. I can't imagine Danielle helping me though.

It's never taken me as long to get down a simple flight of stairs. I'm out of breath by the time we reach the bottom and stand in front of Shaun. I'm better than I was though.

"Well done, Mum." He pats my good arm.

I frown at him and bite my lip. I'm not a pet dog, nor do I

want patronising praise for managing something so small as stairs. I've *got* to get back to normal.

"We'll let you get your breath back before that cup of tea." Leanne leads me towards the chair in the corner of the hallway.

"Is it every other day, that you're coming here to see me Leanne?"

"Yes. If that's OK?" She looks at Shaun.

His expression is vague. "Yes, if that's what Danielle asked for."

"Of course it's OK. I know you can help me get better. And it's lovely to have a friendly and such a pretty face around. Isn't it Shaun?"

"Hmmm, what?"

"Leanne. She's got a pretty face, hasn't she?"

He gives me a look that I can't read.

"Where's Danielle," Leanne asks.

"I'm not sure to be honest. She gave me the impression she wouldn't be here when you came, but didn't give me any clue of where she might be going."

"Maybe she's got another man?" I laugh, but no one else does.

"What do you mean?" Shaun frowns.

"Nothing," I reply in the sweetest voice I can muster.

"Right. Come on Jeannie. Let's help you to the kitchen and we'll see if your tea making is as good as your imagination."

8

***

DANIELLE

"So, how long is Jeannie staying with you?" Mum stirs her coffee as I admire the gorgeous handbag she's bought for me. There won't have been much change out of four hundred pounds, and even the woman at the next table is looking at it. I feel better already, just being in Mum's company, and I really don't want to go home. It's a shame I can't just take the children to my parents and stay there. Shaun would have to do something drastic then. That is if he even noticed I'd gone.

"Hopefully not long. We've arranged for my friend Leanne, who's a physio, to come in and work with Jeannie every other day." I sigh as I glance around the coffee shop at all the people nonchalantly enjoying a coffee. They probably have normal home lives and are not forced to live with someone they don't want to. "The house isn't big enough for both Jeannie and I."

"Aww, she's not that bad Danielle!" Mum chuckles, but I know she's secretly glad I'm far from close to Jeannie, and am not doing nice things with her. I think Mum's also relieved that she does not step on her toes as the children's grandma. Mum does loads with them both and we want to keep it that way. "She's always been perfectly civil in front of me."

"She really *is that bad*. You haven't heard how she speaks to me when it's just me and her." I sip my latte. "What's that expression, she's a wolf in sheep's clothing."

"I thought she'd mellowed in recent years. Yes, everything's lovely thanks." Mum says to the waitress who approaches our table before she's got chance to ask. I would hate to have a job like hers. It must be such a long day.

"No, she's just got sneakier. She plays the 'woe-is-me-little-old-woman' but it's all an act. And Shaun changes when she's around too."

"How do you mean - changes?" Mum places her cup onto her saucer.

"Not only is he cold and distant towards me, which is bad enough, but he regresses into a mummy's boy. It's like she can do no wrong in his eyes." I point at Mum's froth moustache.

She laughs as she brushes it off. "Jeannie's his mother, love. And I'm sure you're imagining him being 'cold and distant' as you put it. He absolutely dotes on you."

"Not anymore. He's changed. I'm so miserable with it all." Tears stab at the backs of my eyes. I'm tired. I haven't slept well for the last few nights. Shaun's not even cuddling up to me in bed like he normally would. Last night, I was on the sofa by two am, and he said nothing this morning. It's not as though I could use our spare room. Not with *her*. "You'll have to come around and see for yourself. And I know she's his mother. I can hardly forget." I wring my hands in my lap. I need my mother on my side, not making excuses for Jeannie. It's bad enough that she's hoodwinking my children. "At one time I could cope with her in small doses, especially when Bob was alive. But I can't cope with having her living at my house." It feels good to be able to talk about what I'm going through at last.

Mum looks deep in thought as though trying to come up with a solution. If only it was that easy. Usually, there's not much my mother can't solve for me.

"Obviously, it would be different if it was you, Mum." I reach for her hand across the table. "If you were ill, I'd bend over backwards to get you better and help look after you. Dad too."

"I know Danielle. You don't even need to say that to me. You're a wonderful daughter and I wouldn't swap you for all the tea in China."

"Thanks Mum." I brush a tear away. "It's been a rubbish few days."

"Jeannie doesn't know how lucky she is, having you as a daughter-in-law." She looks thoughtful again. "I'll come with you to collect the children, shall I?"

"They'd love that." Then I wonder whether we can go somewhere else after collecting them. I still don't want to go home. Not one bit. The atmosphere is awful – certainly no good for the children.

"Careful, you two!" Shaun jumps up as the children launch themselves at Jeannie. I've kept them out for as long as I can. It's not too far away from their bedtime now. I hope they flatten her. He gently manoeuvres them back, away from his mother, as though she's some precious relic in a waxwork museum. If only.

"Where've you all been anyway? School finished hours ago."

"We went out for tea with my Mum at a soft play area." I glance at Jeannie, waiting for her reaction – probably a snarky comment. Perhaps if she'd not spent ten years unfavourably comparing me to Simone and putting everything about me down, I might have taken her along too. She's only herself to blame for the fact that you could not pay me to do anything with her.

"Could you not have let me know you were eating out?" Shaun's eyebrows furrow, like his dad's used to when he wasn't happy. "I've been waiting to put dinner on."

"Since when do I have to report to *you,* Shaun?" I smile and fold my arms. *I'll show you.* "Besides, I thought I'd let you have some quality time with your mother."

"It's called common courtesy." He glares at me. "I've got a lasagne in the oven. It took me ages to make."

"Never mind. You'll just have to dine with your house guest, won't you?" I watch as his expression darkens at how I've just referred to her. I don't care. "What's she doing down here anyway?" As soon as I say the last sentence, I'm only too aware of my rudeness. Even my mum would have a go at me for this, but I carry on anyway. "Who's going to get her back to her room?"

"I will, when she's ready to go back to it, which won't be until later." He sits on the sofa beside her. "I'm so sorry Mum. Take no notice of my ill-mannered wife."

"Don't you be apologising on my account." I avoid looking at Jeannie and instead look back towards the door. I need to get away from her. I can never make eye contact with people I dislike. "She shouldn't be down here – she's supposed to be too unwell to be carrying on as normal. In fact, you can take her back upstairs when you've both eaten."

"How dare you?" Her three anger laden words sound like the old Jeannie. Not a slur anywhere. "I won't let you speak about me like this."

I can't bear the sound of her voice. The children are rooted to the spot, making me feel slightly guilty. They're not used to this sort of animosity. I've probably said too much about the situation to Mum in front of them as well, when we were having dinner, but I had to talk to someone.

Shaun's not listening to me. I'll never forget how he's disregarded my feelings and opinions with this. And how hostile he's become. I don't know how we're ever going to get our marriage back on track.

"Shaun, are you going to let your wife talk to me like this?" She fiddles with the corner of her cardigan as she speaks.

"Oh for God's sakes." He slaps his hand onto the empty cushion on the sofa. Usually, he's only ever exasperated with one of the children. I normally keep my distance from his mother so as not to have these problems. "Both of you. Why can't you just get on? I've had enough of all this. Is it so difficult for you to be civil? For the sake of the children if not for me."

"Shaun, I'm telling you - Danielle can't speak to me like she does. You should hear her when you're not around. I've let Leanne know what's going on." She turns to me. "You just wait."

Ugh. She has drool dripping down her chin. "What do you mean, *you've let Leanne* know what's going on? What lies have you been telling her?"

"Right kids." Shaun points towards the door. "To your rooms please. Pyjamas."

"But it's not bedtime yet Dad."

"I don't care what time it is. I want to speak to your mum and grandma in private, please. Go on."

They scuttle from the room. I feel so bad – this is their home too. For the first time since my arrival back home, I make eye contact with Jeannie, then look at my husband. "I'm sorry Shaun. I shouldn't have started in front of the children."

"You really shouldn't." His mouth is set in a hard, straight line. He's furious, and it's clear he is blaming me, rather than his precious mother. He doesn't look back at me. His eyes are fixed on the TV and his hands are clasped across his chest.

I can't stand his expression. She's really got in between us. "Go on then Jeannie. So how do I speak to you? What have you been telling my friend about me?" God this is awful. Why the hell does it have to be like this? I can tell Shaun is on her side.

It's written all over him. "It's no worse than you've spoken to me all these years."

"I can handle the verbal abuse," she begins. She seems to have forgotten to slur. I knew these so-called after-effects of her so-called stroke were an act. "It's the physical abuse I can't stand." She pulls the neckline down on her nightie to reveal several black dots around her collarbone as she turns to the left. "Have you seen what she's done to me Shaun – she's been prodding me?"

I gasp. "She's lying. She's done that to herself. Shaun! You've got to believe me! You know me better than that!"

Shaun looks as though this revelation has winded him as he stands from the sofa. "Mum. I'm going to take you through to the kitchen and get you started with your dinner." He steps towards her. "The children will keep you company whilst you eat." He turns to me, his voice hardening. "I'll be back to speak to you shortly."

Whilst he's gone, I slip upstairs. I need to find out what I am dealing with before we go any further.

"Leanne. It's Danielle here." I sink onto the bed, my heart thudding inside my chest. It's a sad state of affairs when I've got to sit in my bedroom, in darkness, to have a private conversation.

"Danielle. Oh, hello." I've never heard her sound so sceptical when I've rung her before. She normally sounds pleased to hear from me, but this time, there's no friendliness in her voice. "Is everything OK?"

"I'm sorry to disturb you. I'll get straight to the point. What's my wonderful mother-in-law been saying about me to you?"

"What do you mean?"

For a moment, I wonder if Jeannie is lying. Whether she's said anything to Leanne at all. "Well... you should hear what she's been telling Shaun about me. I'm ringing because she said she's told you the same things as well."

"Such as?"

I try to slow my breath, but I'm panicking. "That I've been speaking to her badly and prodding her in the chest. It's all rubbish, but then, I'm sure you know that. You don't need me to tell you."

There's silence on the other end of the phone, so I continue. I've got to make sure she believes me. Maybe it was a mistake hiring her as Jeannie's physio. But if it had not been Leanne, Jeannie would have peddled her poison to whoever else was available. "If you've seen the bruising on her – around her collarbone, she's done it to herself." I am so stressed. I could be in real trouble here.

"Danielle. I can't repeat anything that Jeannie says to me. It comes down to patient confidentiality, and she's my patient."

"But I arranged it with you. And you only met her for the first time today. Come on Leanne, I thought we were friends."

"It makes no difference. I'm sorry."

She doesn't sound sorry. "You're kidding." I pace along the carpet towards the window. "Has she told you the same thing? Are you going to report me for something I haven't even done?" Oh my God. I knew Jeannie was trouble, but...

"I'm sorry. I just can't comment on this."

"Right, OK. I understand." Hopefully, I can calm Shaun down enough to get through to him. Get him to believe me and find a way forward with him. Once he thinks about it rationally, he'll believe what I tell him – that she's caused her own bruises. But I've got to stay calm and in control of this. "Are you able to tell me your thoughts from assessing her? And when she might be able to go back home?"

Leanne's voice audibly relaxes. Clearly, we're back in safer territory. We're friends. She won't report me for some half-baked allegation a delusional old woman has come out with. "Jeannie's doing well. But she needs support to get up and down the stairs and to get in and out of bed. She's still weak on one side. It won't do her any good to be shut away upstairs on her own either. I gather she's been eating meals in her room?"

I don't respond to the last comment, question, or whatever it is. *What's the point?* Jeannie clearly has not left a stone unturned whilst she has been trying to invite Leanne's sympathy. Perhaps I should have stuck around this morning and not left the situation unattended. "How long do you think she'll need help for?"

"How long is a piece of string? It could be months – definitely weeks."

I can't cope with her for days, let alone weeks. I'm going to have to organise a carer or something. "Do you think she could manage at home if we sorted a care package?"

"Ideally," I detect an edge in Leanne's voice that I haven't heard before, "a stroke victim recovers more quickly with a loving family looking after them. But, in the circumstances..."

"I'll speak to Shaun. Things really aren't working out here." I've never felt heavier as I end the call. Everything's falling apart. And there's only one person to blame.

9

―――――

JEANNIE

So far, so good. I've been here for just over a week, and Leanne is coming for the fourth time today. Danielle and Shaun no longer try to hide their hostility towards each other. It's incredible how quickly their relationship is deteriorating. I can't help but feel that I'm doing my son a huge favour by bringing it to the fore. He'll thank me for it one day.

I'm not sure if he really believes what I've told him about Danielle, but it's certainly planted a seed of doubt in his mind, and that's good enough to be going on with. He's been sneaking around, clearly checking up and listening. He's also had a few low-voiced conversations with Leanne, so hopefully things will progress there.

The worst Shaun and Danielle have been was yesterday morning. I caught snippets of them going at each other.

"Either she goes, or I do!" Danielle had yelled at him, evidently not caring if I heard. The children had come running into my room. We'd listened to them shouting at each other for ten minutes, then the front door had banged and I'd fervently prayed it was Danielle who'd stormed out and not Shaun. My poor grandkids. Bob and I never had a cross word in front of Shaun when he was growing up, which is the way it should be.

It's Monday morning and Shaun is just back from taking the children to school. The sun is seeping around the edges of the curtains, filling me with hope. Danielle has not been back since she slammed out of the house yesterday. It's been absolute heaven. As she was out, I didn't have to pretend I was as incapable as I have been doing, and we had a lovely board game and a film last night. We couldn't have done that if *she'd* been here. While we were eating a Sunday roast around the table, I couldn't help thinking this is what it would be like all the time if my daughter-in-law would just clear off for good. Things are looking promising on that front.

Within moments of the door closing, I hear Shaun's footsteps on the stairs. He appears in the doorway of my room. He's grown into such a fine man and I'm so proud of him. Whatever happens with his marriage, I'll support him. I just want him to find a partner in life who deserves him and looks after him properly. If I could get along with her as well, that would be a huge bonus.

"Right, shall we get you downstairs Mum? You must be ready for some breakfast."

I begin to tug a jumper over my head. "What if *she* comes back? Give me a hand with this, would you love?"

"*Danielle,* you mean? I doubt it. She might do later when the kids are back though." He switches the light off I've left on in the en-suite, then walks towards me. "Anyway, you just concentrate on getting better. Don't worry about Danielle."

"Why does she dislike me so much? I'd do anything for us to be friends."

It's a blatant lie, and I'm sure Shaun knows it too. He gives me a funny look then helps me with my jumper.

"It's true Shaun. Look how well I got on with Simone when you two were together. I'll never get my head around how you blew it with her and for what? Danielle of all people? I warned you it was a mistake."

"Not this old chestnut. How many times? That was years ago. Swing your legs around Mum." He looks around the floor. "Where are your slippers?"

"Simone was lovely. I bet if you'd married her like you were supposed to, she'd have made me welcome in your home. Especially when I'm getting over a stroke." I point to my slippers.

"Well, your speech is improving Mum!" He pulls the curtains open and stands in front of me.

"So have you heard from Danielle since she flounced off yesterday?" I watch his face, half hoping he'll say that he never wants to see or speak to her again. Especially after all the information I've imparted about how she's been behaving towards me. He helps me up, and I slide my feet into my slippers.

"No. But I've spoken to her mother. Danielle turned up there yesterday. It's a good job I took some time off work isn't it? If I'd had to rely on Danielle…" We walk to the bedroom door.

"You can't leave me on my own with your wife Shaun. *If* she comes back I mean." He grips my weaker arm as we shuffle along the carpet towards the top of the stairs.

"She better had come back. I'm supposed to be going clay pigeon shooting tomorrow. I cancelled it last week. I'm meeting a couple of friends."

"You're going to leave me. With *her*. After what I've told you? After what she's done?" I pause and look at him. "You can't!"

"Look. When she comes back, we'll all talk about it. Try to find a way through this."

"*Find a way through this.* You've got to be joking. Look, I'm sorry Shaun." I grip the bannister at the top of the stairs. "I don't mean to be a burden and I don't want to get in the way of what you'd normally do."

"You're not a burden. We'll sort something out."

"Perhaps my neighbour could come and sit with me whilst you're gone. If you really have to go, that is."

"Do you mean Margaret?"

"Yes. She'd keep an eye on me. Danielle might not come back, anyway."

"Is your neighbour around all the time?"

"Ye-es." I say slowly, wondering what he's getting at. "You'd have to pick her up and take her home though."

"Maybe we should be looking at getting you home, Mum, especially with you having someone nearby full time. We could get you a package of care in place too. It's supposed to be really good nowadays."

I sink to the floor of the step we've reached. I can't let Danielle beat me. "But I'd be like a prisoner in my own bedroom. I want to stay here."

"Of course you wouldn't. They'd get you up every day. First thing every morning and then put you to bed whatever time you want to go. That's how it works."

"Put me to bed! I'm a grown woman, for God's sake."

"It's just a thought Mum."

"But I love being around you and the children."

"And we love you being here. It's just – it's not really working out is it? You're not happy. Danielle's not happy. I need to get back to work..."

"You just want to go clay pigeon shooting. I can see straight through you."

"It's not just that. I'm thinking that you going home is for the best now. You're over the worst of things, aren't you? You've done great." He tugs at my arm. "We could visit most days and I could maybe come and stay with you at the weekends. I'd bring the kids as well. Come on Mum, get up."

I allow him to haul me back to my feet. "Yes, like Danielle would allow you to come and stay with me. She's so controlling over you and the children. I've never seen anything like it."

"Only because I used to allow her to be. I'm trying to change things. You must have seen that."

"I don't know how you stand for it."

"I know. Anything for a quiet life."

"Just like your father." I feel almost teary. It really sounds as though I'm going to be sent back to my poky flat.

"There's nothing wrong with wanting a quiet life, is there?"

"I really miss him Shaun."

"Who – Dad? I know. So do I. Come on. You're nearly halfway down. Keep going."

"I don't want to be on my own." I sink to the step again. "I really want to stay here. Look, I'll try harder with Danielle. I'll do anything." I brush a tear away with my sleeve.

"You shouldn't have to. Let's just get you sat downstairs and *then* we can talk about it. I didn't mean to upset you."

I watch from the kitchen table as Shaun chops fruit for me and spoons yoghurt on top of it. I've calmed down, but need to think of a way forward that doesn't involve me returning home. Not yet.

"Get that down you Mum. Do you want a cup of tea?" His voice echoes around the spacious kitchen. It's three times the size of mine. He's done so well for himself. Especially considering how bone idle his wife is.

"I don't know what I'd do without you love." I pick up the spoon with my good hand.

"You're doing well Mum. You'll be able to manage better than you expect, honestly."

"You're not listening to me are you Shaun? I said I'll try harder with Danielle. I'll stay in my room more." I put my spoon down. "Please don't make me go back to my flat love. Not yet. I can't face it. Not after what happened last time I was there." As if I am begging and pleading with my own son like this.

"Look." He shuts the fridge door and turns to face me. "You can see what you staying here is doing to my marriage. It's not that I'm blaming you – of course I'm not, Danielle has got a hell of a lot to answer for. It just..."

"What?" He's going to make me go back. My plan has fallen apart before it has even begun.

"I can't keep allowing the children to overhear what they're having to overhear from us all. It's not fair. They're not happy." He takes two mugs from the cupboard.

"But it's not me causing the trouble or the arguments. It's your wife." I can't eat my breakfast now. I've totally lost my appetite.

"You forget Mum. I've heard you *both* over the years, you and Danielle, and I'm sick of being stuck in the middle of it. I've told Danielle the same. You need to sort it out."

"This is what your wife does." I roll up the sleeve on my dressing gown to show the bruising on the wrist of my good arm. "She sticks *you* in the middle of things. "

"That's because I've allowed her so far to stick me there." He carries on making cups of tea, rather than commenting on my arm. "But not anymore."

It's time to fire my bullets. "Do you know she's threatened to stop me seeing Benny and Gem-Gem again? *For ever*, she said. I don't think you really know who you're dealing with Shaun." I push my bowl away. "Someone who's capable of threatening to stop your children seeing their own grandmother."

"Danielle's just a bit spoilt. She's had a lifetime of getting her own way and she's been given everything she wants – we know that. I don't think she means most of what she says. She just speaks without thinking." He takes hold of my arm at last. "That looks nasty? What have you been doing?"

"Saturday. When you'd taken the children shopping." Here we go.

"But Leanne was here. I purposely waited until after she had got here before we set off."

I snatch my arm back and make a meal of rubbing at it. "She wasn't here the whole time though."

"So what happened?"

"I'd told Leanne the latest. I've got to talk to *someone* Shaun. Your wife is making my life a misery." He appears to hang his head. I feel certain that he believes me.

"Anyway, I heard Leanne and Danielle talking in the hallway for a while, then, when Leanne had gone, Danielle came upstairs, grabbed my wrist and asked me why I keep lying about her. But I'm not. I haven't. It really hurts."

Shaun sinks to a chair opposite me. He looks exhausted. Who'd have thought a little thing like me coming to convalesce at my son's house for a month could cause so much trouble?

"What exactly have you told Leanne Mum? I need to know."

"And I need you to deal with your wife. Leanne already knew what had happened last week. About Danielle prodding me in the chest and making me stay upstairs, I mean."

He sighs and folds a newspaper into quarters. "Go on."

"Before you'd even set off on Saturday, Danielle was making threats about getting Power of Attorney and getting me put into a care home."

"When? Where was I? I haven't been leaving the two of you on your own."

"Downstairs. You were getting the children sorted before you went shopping."

"You know as well as I do, Danielle can't get Power of Attorney. You're my mother, not hers. Why did you even take it on board?"

"That's what I told her. We were arguing about it and then she threw tea into my face." I look down at my hands.

"You're joking Mum." He drops his head into his hands. *"She threw tea in your face?"*

"She said, *whoops, never mind. My hand slipped.* Look, you can still see all the tea here." I point at the front of the beige skirt I am wearing. "Thank God it had cooled down. She could have really scalded me."

"That'll be Leanne." Shaun rises from his chair in response to the doorbell. "I'll let her in." I watch as he walks to the door and ducks under the frame. He's taller than his Dad was but not as feisty. I know that if I'd have said a word against Bob's Mum, ever, Bob would have shot me down in flames. Besides, I wouldn't have dared. I had far too much respect for her.

Danielle has never had one iota of respect for me. Which is why it's almost a pleasure to watch my son's expression as he grows to learn exactly what his wife is capable of. I can only hope he acts on it. I don't know where it's going to leave us if he doesn't. Surely Leanne's formal intervention will mean he has to. I'm going to take this all the way. A proper complaint against Danielle if that's what I have to do. The only place I want to see her face is across a court room.

Shaun and Leanne are talking in low voices again in the hallway. I can't make out what they're saying. And I'm obviously not supposed to. I'll tell her what's happened since I last saw her on Saturday. Show her the latest bruising. I'm so pleased now that Danielle arranged a physiotherapist for me. And to think it peeved me to start with. Leanne has got a duty of care towards me. Imagine if I died or something, and she'd known all along of the risk that Danielle posed. She couldn't risk her career in that way.

10

DANIELLE

"Why don't you like Grandma Mum?"

It doesn't make me feel good, hearing Gemima come out with that, clear as day. My children shouldn't be having to deal with what's going on between us so-called grown-ups. Why the hell couldn't Shaun have respected my wishes?

"Who says I don't like Grandma?" I glance at her in the rear-view mirror.

"She told us. And we've heard you shouting at each other. I don't like it, it makes me sad and scared when people shout."

"Our house isn't happy anymore Mum." Oh God, it must be bad for Benedict to chime in. "I told Mrs Knight about it. She said I was being quiet at school when usually I make too much noise. She asked me what was wrong."

"You did what?" Raising my voice isn't the best course of action in the circumstances, but it sounds as though I'm being totally blamed for this mess by Leanne, by Shaun, and now by my own children. I can't believe that even the school knows there are problems at home. There weren't any until *she* arrived and took everything over. I bet she loved me being out of the way last night and would make that a permanent arrangement if she could. That's what she has wanted all along. My husband. My children. My home. My life. She's warped. She needs more help than a *physiotherapist* can offer her.

I pull over and swing around to look at Benedict. He hangs his head. "I'm sorry Mum. But it's true. Everyone keeps shouting and Grandma was crying yesterday. I had to give her a hug to make her feel better."

I stare at his dear little face, knowing I've got to sort this – and fast. Maybe I should get some legal advice. It's looking that way.

"Tell her what else Mrs Knight said Ben." Gemima's plaits swing with her as she turns in the passenger seat to look at Benedict. There's an edge to her voice which suggests she's enjoying her moment of imparting important information to me.

Ben, in contrast, looks worried. "Mrs Knight was having a staff meeting today, but she wants to speak to you tomorrow. Am I in trouble Mum?"

"Oh, great." I immediately decide to let Shaun pick them up from school tomorrow. It's his bloody mother, and he's the one who has caused all this. I said I didn't want Jeannie to stay – with very good reason as it's turning out, but Shaun completely ignored me. He can deal with the fallout and the embarrassment of being hauled in after school.

I'm surprised to find Shaun loitering outside when I pull up on the drive. He doesn't appear to be doing anything – just waiting and moving gravel about with his foot. Perhaps he's come to his senses and wants to talk to me. He's quiet as we all get out, his hands thrust in his pockets. I ache for him suddenly. I can't even remember the last time he told me he loved me.

"Inside kids," he says as soon as we're all out of the car, nudging them towards the door. "Go and watch TV with your Grandma. She's in the lounge. I need to speak to your mother."

His tone of voice suggests he means business. Gemima gives

me a knowing look I've seen too often lately. She takes hold of Benedict's hand and they scuttle inside, their feet crunching against the gravel as they go. I notice Jeannie watching us from the window, her face pale in the shadows, but wearing a smug expression. I'd love to make it disappear. I'd love to make *her* disappear.

"So what do you want?" I try to meet my husband's gaze, but he looks down at his feet.

He pauses, then raises his eyes to mine. "I don't want you here right now Danielle." His voice is low and uncertain. He glances towards where his mother is peering from the window at us. "You've got ten minutes to pack whatever you need and leave."

"Eh? You can't... what are you on about?" Fear clutches me. Has it really come to this?

"We need some space to sort out what's gone wrong here. I need some space. We can't go on like this. None of us can." He thrusts his hands deeper into his pockets. Under normal circumstances, I'd hug him. He looks thoroughly miserable.

I follow his gaze to the lounge window. "Look, I'm not having this conversation with *her* watching on." I can't believe what she's done to us.

"Fine." Shaun strides towards the back garden and I chase after him. He stops next to the pond. We've spent many a summer evening here, with a glass of wine in hand, putting the world to rights. It's unthinkable how much our relationship has crumbled.

"What's going on Shaun. Why have you let your mother do this to us? I told you all along that she shouldn't stay here."

He swings around to face me, anger sparking from his eyes. "What have *you* done to my mother, you mean?"

I close my eyes against the awful expression he's wearing for a moment. "Whatever she's told you about me, she's totally lying. You've got to believe me. Shaun. Come on. I'm your wife.

You know me." I feel the heat of tears ready to erupt. I've felt like this more in the last couple of weeks than I have in my entire life.

He grabs me by the wrist. It's the first time he's ever laid a hand on me. "I've seen the bruising, here on her wrist. How would you like it if I did that to you?" He holds my wrist in front of my face, and I find myself wondering if the neighbours are listening to all this on the other side of the fence.

"Get off, you're hurting me." I try to tug my arm away.

"The bruising around her collarbone and the grab marks on her upper arms. You're an utter bitch Danielle. I've half a mind to report you to the police myself." He lets my arm fall. "I haven't decided what to do for the best yet."

"Does Leanne think I've done all that too?" Leanne and I have been friends for years. I should never have got her involved in this situation. I thought it would speed up Jeannie's return home. If I can just get Leanne to believe me...

"It was Leanne that Mum confided in. She didn't want me to know. Thank God she had someone she felt she could talk to. And who knows what else you might have been capable of if you hadn't been stopped." He walks away from me, towards the pond. This garden is our happy place. I cannot believe we're stood here, having a conversation like this.

"She's lying," I repeat, my voice quieter this time. "Do you really think I'd risk getting into trouble for *her*?" I'm absolutely done for here. "Or that I'd risk losing you Shaun." The tears are coursing down my cheeks now. I can't get my head around him believing her over me. She really is trying to wreck our family.

"Not only have you been violent Danielle, she's told me what you've been saying to her."

"As if you believe what's coming out of her poisonous mouth over your own wife."

He walks back towards me. "You've been making threats that she won't see the children again, and threats about putting her into a care home. I'd like to know how you think you could effect that." He thrusts his hands into his pockets, poison dripping from his words. I've never seen him like this before. "She's my mother, Danielle. If and when she's ever without capacity, I'll be the one making the decisions, not you."

"I've told you Shaun. She's giving you her own version of events. I've never said anything of the sort. She's trying to cause trouble – to get in between us."

"Oh, she's done that alright." He raises his voice. "I want you out. My mother isn't safe around you. That's the bottom line here."

"This is my house as much as yours. Take her home if you don't want to be around me. *The lying bitch.* You can't make me go anywhere."

"You either go quietly or I'll make you go." His jaw is clenched.

"And how do you propose to do that?" I'm braced to fight back if he goes for me again, but I still step back instinctively.

We stand facing each other like two sworn enemies, not a loving married couple with two children and a beautiful home. We're panting like dogs with unspent stress and anger. I know, deep down, that I'm going to have to spend at least another night at my parent's house. But I can't stay here. He's not going to let me – there's just no getting through to him. God knows what's going to happen to me now. I could be in serious trouble. Oh God, what if I lose my kids because of it? Leanne will be duty bound to file a report. Jeannie has even come between us as friends.

I stand in the centre of the garden, my thoughts whirling with the wintery breeze, feeling as desolate as the surrounding grey sky. It's as though my whole world is closing in. Why couldn't Shaun have listened to me? I know what Jeannie is capable of – why can't he see it? No wonder my heckles rose when he told me she was coming to stay.

The tears won't stop. I wipe them on my coat sleeves. There's no way I'm going to get him to believe me over her. I'm going to have to confront her. Make her change her story. By whatever means possible. I stride towards the conservatory with Shaun hot on my heels. He obviously thinks I'm going to get a few things together, as instructed, and go quietly. He can think again.

11

JEANNIE

I JUMP as Danielle storms into the lounge. She has an expression on her face that both frightens me and excites me in equal measure. It's all about to blow up. I'm flanked either side by Benny and Gem-Gem. Hopefully, the sight of us all cosying up will enrage Danielle even more. Now what I need is for her to go for me in front of Shaun. Their marriage is hanging by a thread, and her attacking me in front of the children will surely snap that thread completely. It will be worth a few more bruises.

"I thought you were leaving dear."

"Don't you ever call me *dear*. And I'm going nowhere. If anyone is leaving this house, *my* house, it's going to be *you*." She comes towards me.

"Mum. Please don't talk like this to Grandma. I really don't like it." I've never heard such desperation in my granddaughter's voice.

I pull Gemima closer into me. Any minute Shaun will burst into the room and send the children packing. I hope he stalls for a few moments as it's important that they see their mother in action. If they're aware of what she's capable of, they'll understand her departure better. It will be easier for them to get over.

"Shaun said you were leaving. You're supposed to be packing, aren't you?"

"Shaun's wrong. I'm going nowhere. Like I said, you're the one who's going Jeannie. I mean it." She comes closer to us and bends down. "Enough is enough."

I've never seen such ugliness in a person's face. Hopefully the children will come to know it too. Goodness knows why my son ever married her.

"I didn't want you here in the first place," she continues. "You're a lying bitch and you're trying to poison my family against me. You're leaving. Today."

"Mummy that's a naughty word!" Benedict gasps and grips my arm. "Grandma! Please, will you both stop it. Please!"

"You two. To your rooms. Now!" As predicted, Shaun appears in the doorway.

The children release their grasp on me and head for the door, heads bowed as they squeeze past their father. Benedict looks back at us. This is awful for them, but will be worth it in the long run. I've heard Shaun and Leanne laughing together and getting on really well over the last few days. It's only a matter of time...

"Danielle. I said I wanted you to get some things together." His voice is calmer than I would have expected. He's like his dad was though and once his temper goes, it really goes. He's doing well to hang onto it.

She steps in front of him and the defiance in her voice angers me even more. "Make me." She deserves a good slap.

"I don't want this any more than you do," he replies. "But after what you've done to my..."

"Tell him the truth Jeannie." She marches back towards me. "Tell him what a bloody liar you are. Why are you even doing this to me? You're evil. I welcome you into my home, and..."

"Welcome!" I laugh. "Do you know what lady? You don't deserve my son, my grandchildren, or this house. You're lazy, you're spoilt, and he should never..." She lunges at me. "Argh, get away from me." Her grip tightens on my throat. I gurgle within the force of it, yet excitement also courses through me. She's done exactly what I wanted.

Shaun darts towards us and unhooks her fingers from around my neck. My good hand shoots towards it. Amidst my coughing fit, I notice Shaun dragging her back and pushing her into a chair. He swipes his phone from the mantlepiece.

"I'm sorry." Danielle cries, sitting forward as though she's going to get back to her feet. Mascara runs down her face. "I lost it. Anyone would. She's nothing but a liar." She drops her head into her hands. "I'll go. Please don't ring the police."

"Sit back down." Shaun then looks at me, as though to approve this. I shake my head, my hand still clasped to my neck. "Ring them," I say. "Even if you don't want to press charges against her, I do. She's not getting away with that."

"No Shaun, please...Please don't do this to me."

"I don't know you anymore." He presses the phone to his ear. "I can't allow or let you get away with what you've done to my mother. Police please."

She looks at me. "You wait Jeannie." She's crying but she speaks to me through gritted teeth. "You're going to pay for all this. You just wait."

"Have you heard her?" I shriek as I look at Shaun, grim-faced on the phone. "She's still threatening me. Get her away from me." I roll my sleeves up so my bruised wrists are fully on display, then I feel around my neck. That will be coming up too.

"They're on the way. Right you." He grabs Danielle's arm and hoists her to her feet. "We'll wait for them in the hallway. I want you as far away as possible from my mother."

"I can't believe you've called the police on your own wife."

She shakes herself out of his grip, her hair sticking to the sides of her face. "What sort of man are you?"

"What did you think I was going to do?"

I'm pleased to see he has her by the wrist, just in case she has any more thoughts of flying at me again. She's done what I wanted. I don't need a round two.

"Will you be alright on your own for a few minutes Mum? I'll wait in the hallway. When the police get here, they'll need to speak to you as well."

"I'll be fine love. They'll probably need the photos of all my bruising too." My hand flits from my neck, back to my wrist.

"You should be on stage with your skills as an actress," Danielle snarls at me as Shaun leads her from the room. "You just bloody wait."

I watch as a police car pulls up behind Danielle's car on the drive, a male and a female officer get out. The window is open, so I hear their footsteps crunch towards the porch. I hold my breath as the doorbell echoes along the hallway. As it's a well-built thirties semi, I can't make out what's being said, I can only hear muffled voices and the beep of what must be their radios.

Moments later, the children appear in the lounge again, their little faces streaked with tears.

"Grandma." Benny throws himself at me. "I'm scared."

For a moment, I feel guilty for my part in all this but quickly remind myself that I'm doing everyone a favour in the long run. "Come here." I pull him close and Gem-Gem follows him. This will be a day they won't forget in a hurry.

"What's happening Grandma. Why are the police here? They can't take my mum away, can they? Not just for shouting. Please tell them not to take her," Benny sobs.

"It was a bit more than just shouting, sweetie. I don't know what's going to happen. But we'll find out soon. It will all be OK."

Within minutes another police car pulls up, as Danielle is

being led from the house. The two sets of police officers pass on the drive. One of the neighbours is on his drive, washing his car. He stares at Danielle. She's always been overly concerned with what the neighbours think. What everyone thinks. Apart from me of course. This will be crucifying her.

The children are beside themselves when Shaun reappears in the lounge.

"Right kids," he begins. "I want you to put a film on in the playroom. Then as soon as we've finished speaking to the police, we'll all go out. Do something nice."

"But I want my Mum." Gemima is sobbing now, having watched her being led away.

"Poor little thing." I stroke the top of her head. "It will all feel better soon. I promise. You go with your brother. We won't be long."

12

DANIELLE

I blink as I become re-accustomed to my surroundings. I must have fallen asleep. They've let me ring Mum and there's a solicitor on the way. I shiver and pull the scratchy blanket up to my chin.

I haul myself up to sitting and momentarily close my eyes against the brick walls, stone floor and metal toilet in the corner. This can't be happening. The terrified faces of Gemima and Benedict swim into my mind. What have we done to them? How will we ever get beyond this?

I refuse the offering of a meal brought in by one of the officers but accept the watery tea in a plastic cup. There's no way I would eat the muck they serve up in here. I couldn't stop crying when I was initially locked in, but feel too shocked to cry now. It's as though there are no tears left.

"I'd like a few moments with my client before we get started, please."

"Very well." The stern-faced female officer who led me from my home points us into a box-like room.

Lindsey Walker, the criminal law solicitor Mum has

appointed for me, introduces herself, then reaches around the doorway to the room and the fluorescent lighting flickers on. It makes my eyes ache after the gloom of the cell I've been in for what feels like hours. I don't even know what time it is, but it's pitch black outside. I think of my children and ache to be with them, cooking their tea and listening to them practising their reading.

Lindsey gestures to one of the seats fastened to the floor. The room is airless with a faint whiff of body odour combined with stale tobacco smoke. My stomach twists around itself with stress, misery and hunger. All around me are the same brick walls as in the cell. Any longer in there and I might have ended up banging my head against them. I'm getting to a point where I can't take any more. I hope to God they let me out after interviewing me.

Right now, there doesn't feel much point in going on with anything. It feels as though my life is over. Everyone is thinking the worst of me, especially my husband who once loved me more than life itself, so he said. Jeannie is covered in marks and bruises, and I'm in serious trouble.

"Right," Lindsey says. "I've spoken to your Mum. She's told me everything she knows about the last couple of weeks."

"She believes me, doesn't she?" As if I could ever doubt Mum. I remember her telling me as a teenager that no matter what, she'd always be my greatest ally and would forever have my back.

"Of course, but as I'm sure you can imagine, she's extremely concerned. Not just about you, but your children as well."

My head droops at this reminder. All was OK until Jeannie turned up. We were a happy family. I've hated her since she tried to sabotage our wedding. She had initially said she wasn't coming, and when that failed to bring her whatever reaction she might have wanted from Shaun, she pretended she was me, and tried to cancel some bookings. Thankfully, I got wind of it when the vicar rang Shaun.

Before that happened, I'd tried everything to win her over. She'd *always* hated me, and I seriously couldn't understand why. Since then, I've done my best to keep my distance from her. But that's not what I'm facing now. This is much worse.

"Your parents are covering my costs Danielle." Lindsey's voice jolts me from my miserable thoughts. "But I need you to sign here to authorise me to act for you."

I sign my name, wondering whether I'll be called it for much longer, or whether Shaun will end up divorcing me after what his mother is accusing me of. I suppose he's duty bound to protect her first.

"I'm going to come straight out with it," Lindsey begins, her bracelets rattling, as she tucks her red hair behind one ear. "Are you guilty of what they've alleged against you?"

"Not the physical part of things. The bruising and all that." I sniff. "Apart from today when she riled me – I went for her. I totally lost it when my husband was kicking me out of the house. In front of my children as well. I hold my hands up to that. I was totally wrong no matter how much she provoked me."

"OK. Well it's likely you'll be facing a charge for what's happened today. But we'll go through what led to it in interview, and then we'll talk privately again at the end."

"I'm guilty of some of the things I've *said* to her whilst she's been staying with us. Things like not wanting her there, and threats not to let her see the children. But after how she's treated me over the years, she had an absolute nerve turning up at my home in the first place, expecting me, of all people, to look after her."

The solicitor is scribbling things down as I speak, and I wonder what she must think of me. I hope she believes me.

"And what about the allegations of physical injury prior to today?"

"She's done all of it to herself. It's a calculated effort to get me out of the family home, I think."

"Right." She takes a deep breath. "If that's the case, I'm going to advise you to answer the interview questions honestly and most importantly, calmly. If there's anything you're not sure about, just ask. You can also ask to speak to me alone if you need to. I'm confident," she continues, "that we should be able to get police bail for you. It's unlikely that you'll be able to go back home though. I'd imagine staying away will be part of your bail conditions."

"You're joking. But my children..." Panic clutches at my chest as I envisage being kept away from them. This has never happened for more than two nights before and is really going to give the mums at the school gates something to talk about.

"Are the children in your husband's care?"

"Yes, but *she's* there too. My mother-in-law. And she'll poison them against me more than she already has. There's no bail to protect my children from that, is there?" Suddenly there's shouting and banging in the custody area outside our interview room and I find myself wondering for the millionth time, how the hell I ended up in here. If anyone had suggested to me a month ago that I'd be in this predicament now, I'd have laughed at them.

"OK Danielle. Well, as you know, I'm a criminal law specialist, but I'll put you in touch with Lisa, our family law specialist tomorrow. She'll help sort out the situation with regard to your children, depending on what happens here today. Don't worry, between Lisa and myself, we'll get you the very best outcome – whatever it takes."

"You *will* get me out of here today, won't you?" I suddenly panic, imagining being made an example of. Being led away and locked up, pending trial. No bail. Jeannie will have put on her best act. Like I said, she should be on stage.

"Yes. Just remain calm and don't give them a reason to detain you."

It's the first time I have ever been inside a police station, let alone a cell or an interview room. I'm almost too numb to be angry as two police officers take their seats in front of me. The words of the rights that are read out to me swim through and around my thoughts, and for a moment, I feel as though I could pass out. It's almost like I'm having an out-of-body experience and watching myself from the outside. I'm beyond stressed with it all and have got to get out of here. But I can do this. I can get through it. And the solicitor seems to know what she's doing. I've just got to trust her.

Mum's waiting in the car in the car park as I emerge from the police station an hour later. She jumps out of the car as soon as she sees me.

"Oh Danielle. Are you alright love?" She holds her arms out and pulls me in.

I wrap my arms around her, relief washing over me. "It's nothing that a glass of wine wouldn't fix." Thank God I've got my mother. "Can you take me for one Mum?"

"Jump in. I could do with one myself. I've been worried sick about you for the last few hours."

"They've taken my photo, my DNA, my fingerprints, they've locked me in a cell." I drop my chin to my chest and shake my head. "They've treated me like a proper criminal. I can't believe it Mum."

"Neither can I, but it's over with for now. You're out of there love." She lets me go and walks around to the driver's side. "Let's get a glass of wine down us. I'll get your dad to collect us."

"Thanks for sorting the solicitor." I look at her across the roof of the car and try to smile. "She was really good."

"At least she got bail for you." We get into the car and Mum pulls the seatbelt across herself. "I was really worried, given what you've been accused of. Jeannie is seventy-two when all's said and done." I search Mum's face, looking for anything in it that might indicate her thinking that I could have done what I'm being accused of. She keeps her eyes forward and her expression is difficult to read.

"Can I stay with you for a few days Mum? I can't go home, even if I wanted to." Now I'm with her, I can fall apart. She'll put me back together like she always has. I wipe my tears away with the back of my hand.

"Of course you can." She pats my arm. "Your father is disgusted with it all. We can't believe the situation with Jeannie has driven you out of your own home. Where do you want to go?"

Thank God. They are on my side. Relief washes over me like a wave. "To the first pub we get to. Part of my bail conditions are that I cannot contact her, directly or indirectly – any of them. I don't know what I'm going to do about the children."

"Oh my God. Can't she just go home?"

"I'm going to try and speak to Shaun again. I've got to get him to see how she's engineered this."

"Are you allowed to? Have they actually charged you with anything?"

"Yes – they've charged me. I've to report back there in a week. But I will prove myself innocent if it's the last thing I do."

"What have they charged you with?"

"Three counts of actual bodily harm. I grabbed her today Mum. I've been such an idiot. I played right into her hands. Shaun was ordering me to leave and Jeannie wouldn't stop goading me. But that's the only time I've laid hands on her, not like she's making out. She's been playing the victim, and it's all lies. You believe me, don't you Mum?" I search her face again for doubt and am relieved not to find any.

"Of course I do. And in any case, that woman is enough to drive anyone to anything. We'll get you through this love. We'll get you back home."

13

JEANNIE

"IT's so good to hear from you Margaret." I close the door to my bedroom so I can speak in private. "I've had a hell of a few days – I can't tell you how lovely it is to hear a friendly voice."

"Why? I thought you'd be happy staying with your son and grandchildren. Aren't you baking cakes for them by now? What's going on?"

"I'll come to all that in a minute. First, I wanted to check my flat is OK. Have you been keeping an eye on things for me?" I can picture Margaret. She'll be wearing her housecoat. She's a few years older than me, but still dyes her hair. I couldn't be bothered with all that. Thankfully, my hair turned a fabulous silvery shade, which even Bob said he liked.

"Of course I have. I said when I came to the hospital to see you, didn't I? The most exciting thing that's happened is you've had a parcel delivered."

"Good. Thanks. That will be the shirts I ordered for Shaun. The one he was wearing when he last visited the flat was looking rather shabby."

"Hasn't he got a wife for all that?"

"Sore point. I'll tell you about it soon. The flat's OK though? Nothing's gone off, or anything?"

"Everything's fine. I locked up after you were taken in. And yes, I've sorted your fridge and bins."

"Thanks. You're a true friend. And, like I said, I really appreciate what you did for me that day." I walk to the window and absently notice the couple next door getting into their car. It makes me think of when Bob and I used to go out for the day. We would pack up a flask and sandwiches. I was truly living back then. Not like now.

"It's no problem Jeannie. You'd do the same for me."

"Of course I would." I take a deep breath. She's not going to like my next announcement. "Though, I want to give you fair warning, Margaret, that you might be getting a new neighbour to replace me soon. With a bit of luck, I might not be back home. It looks as though I'm going to make a permanent home here, so I'll be able to put my flat on the market." I watch as the neighbours pull out of the driveway, and imagine making friends with them, once things settle down.

"Really. Are you not getting any better? I thought you were doing well when I saw you."

"I'm getting stronger every day as it happens." I open and close the fist on my weaker arm, suddenly remembering my physio exercises. "I've got a lovely physio coming here to see me - Leanne. She's the spit of Simone, you know, the girl Shaun was once engaged to. I mentioned all that, didn't I?"

"Erm, yes." Margaret laughs. "Several times."

"Anyway, I reckon Leanne might become a lasting fixture around here – she's getting on very well with my son."

"Eh? What about his wife?" I picture Margaret, pacing around in front of her lounge window like she always does when on the phone. Much as I miss her, I don't miss my old life.

"She won't be around for much longer."

My eyes fall on the wedding photo resting on the dresser. I

walk towards it and turn it face down. I've been meaning to do that for days. What a pig of a day their wedding day was. Having to pretend to be happy for them. Danielle said at the time I was lucky to be there, and it was only for Shaun's sake that she'd allowed me to be. I admit, tampering with their bookings was reckless, but I expect Danielle would do the same for Benny when he's older. Particularly if he were about to make the biggest mistake of his life.

"Not if I've got anything to do with it. His wife isn't allowed to come back here at the moment. Not since yesterday. She's on police bail."

"What?" I can hear the desperation to find out why in her voice. Margaret has always enjoyed a bit of gossip. She has a quiet, some might say, *dull*, life. *"Bailed?* What's been going on?"

"Hang on a minute." I walk to the bedroom door and check up and down the landing. The house is in silence. Shaun's in his office. With him being in IT, it's too easy for him to log in and get embroiled in work, even when he's on leave. But he must be good at his job to finance the lifestyle they have. Still, everyone needs a break once in a while. His father was a workaholic too.

At least Shaun took some time for himself this morning and went clay pigeon shooting, as he'd wanted to. I think that was the only reason he had any doubts about sending Danielle packing. He said when he came back, that getting out on a shoot with his friends had done him good – he's been so stressed, especially after what happened yesterday.

"OK, what I'm going to tell you is top secret Margaret. You can never tell a soul, do you promise?" I close the bedroom door.

"How long have we been friends Jeannie? Have I ever betrayed your trust? I just want to help, if I can."

I'd like to keep in touch with Margaret after the flat is sold. I knew her well before I moved in there from when she was a judge for the Gorgeous Gardens Competition. Which I never won. Sometimes I wish I'd never let our family home go. It's just, at the time, the memories of Bob were crucifying me. "No, you never have. Or me, yours. There's not much help you can give me with this one though. But listening to me is help enough."

"We've carried some deep, dark secrets for each other over the years, haven't we?"

I laugh then. "This one might even trump that one of yours with the carer."

"Gosh, it must be bad. Let's have it then."

"It might give you a few ideas with your own daughter-in-law. You're always saying you can't stand her."

"True. Although things have been better lately. Come on then. The suspense is killing me."

I'm quite enjoying keeping her dangling. I do miss having a proper chat with people. Shaun has never been the conversational sort, and Danielle, well, she prefers to throttle me. Now that it looks as though I'll be staying here long term, I'll have to integrate myself into the local community and find out what's out there for the over seventies. Not that I usually feel over seventy. Apart from lately. "Well, obviously I didn't plan on having a stroke," I tell Margaret, "but it's safe to say that I've turned it into an opportunity. Every cloud, and all that." I take the photograph I turned over and slide it into a drawer. I want it totally out of my sight. Danielle probably only stood it there to wind me up.

"Go on." The anticipation in Margaret's voice is palpable.

"Well, it was obvious from the word go that she didn't want me here – she's made no secret of it." A vision of Danielle's twisted face jumps into my mind. I blink it away.

"Oh, I'm sorry to hear that. You suspected that might be the case, when I visited you, even though your Shaun had told you differently."

"I know. But he was lying. I'm sure he had his reasons. Anyway, wait until I tell you how I've got back at her."

"Really?"

I should have been a storyteller. I know how to engage people with my words. "She'd have locked me in this room and forgotten about me given half a chance, Danielle would." I look around. It's a nice enough room, but in the first few days, it was like a prison cell. So it's ironic that she ended up in one herself yesterday. Hopefully, she'll know what I've felt like now. "She's been rude to the point of being abusive."

"She definitely sounds in the same league as our Tim's wife. Nice as pie in front of him, but nasty when no one's listening. When you've told me what's been going on for you, I must tell you of her latest escapade."

"So anyway, I decided to teach the lovely Danielle a lesson. As I bruise like a peach these days, it's been easy to gain a few extra." I perch on the edge of the bed. It's so much comfier than my bed at home. My sleep has been much better since I've been here. "My physio, Leanne, seemed to guess it was Danielle causing the bruises before I even told her. I was surprised at this actually, as they're supposed to be friends."

"How come your physio is friends with your daughter-in-law? That doesn't sound like a wise arrangement."

"Danielle arranged for this Leanne one to come every other day. The hospital had only arranged for a weekly visit from an NHS physio. That's how desperate she was to get me back on my feet and out of her house."

"Your daughter-in-law sounds awful. I haven't liked the look of her on the odd occasion I've seen her at your flat, Jeannie. She's got trouble written all over her."

"Leanne also seemed informed about how much Danielle hadn't wanted me here in the first place, and how desperately she wanted me gone. She tried to stick up for Danielle at first, but I could tell it was an act. Though it's all worked in my favour, eventually."

"I can't imagine why she's so negative towards you Jeannie. You're such a lovely person."

I smile. It's always nice to hear something positive. Compliments are few and far between since Bob died. "Thanks Margaret. Although I don't feel so lovely at the moment." I've got a small amount of conscience prickling at me. "I'll get over it though."

"Get over what?"

"I've done the bruising myself. Prodding and grabbing my arms and collar area. I had to do *something*." I walk back across my room towards the window. I can't sit still today. "I made it look like it was Danielle. She was in enough trouble for that anyway, but now..."

"Go on. What's happened?"

"Well, my plan was working. Shaun had told Danielle to stay with her mum for a few days as he believed she was hurting me. He said he wanted time to work out what he was going to do." I fiddle with the hem of the flowery curtains as I speak. There's a lovely view across the fields from this window. It's what I'll be getting used to. Much better than that poky flat. "So anyway, she went for me. In front of the kids and everything. I thought she was going to strangle me. Now she's done that, I do feel better about making the rest of it up."

"Oh my God! When did that happen?"

"Yesterday afternoon. It was awful. Shaun rang the police and had her arrested. She's been charged and is on police bail not to come anywhere near me or the house. It's heaven knowing she can't come back."

"Are you OK?"

"Of course I am. It's all been worth it. There's no way my son would stay with a woman who's capable of manhandling and abusing his mother. And he saw her with his own eyes yesterday. I really was feeling a smidgen, just a smidge mind, guilty at inflicting the bruising on myself. But she's shown her true colours..."

My words catch in my throat as I hear movement within the en-suite. I freeze. "I've got to go Margaret. I'll ring you back shortly."

"What is it? Are you OK?"

I don't reply. Instead, I toss the phone on the bed and reach for the handle of the en-suite door. Sure enough, Shaun is behind it, sat on the shower seat.

"Hello Mum."

I study his face, searching for knowledge of how much of the conversation he's heard. "What are you doing in here?"

"I was fixing the shower door, like you asked me to the other day. But then I heard you come in and begin your conversation. It's a good job I quietly stuck around, isn't it?"

I scan his expression. It's very difficult to read. "How dare you listen in to my private conversations?"

"It's a good thing I did. How could you Mum?" He raises his gaze from the tiled floor to my face.

"How could I what?" I need to think of something quick, to get me out of this. *Damn.* I should have double checked he was in his office. How could I have been so careless?

"All the lies you've told Leanne about Danielle. Not just Leanne. Me. The bloody police."

"You saw yesterday what your wife's capable of Shaun. She might have strangled me if you hadn't intervened." I step towards him. "Come on. We can sort this out, can't we?"

"Stay away from me Mum. I wasn't there at the beginning of whatever went on yesterday to know what you said or did to provoke her. In front of our kids - your *grandkids.* Mum? Why?"

At the moment, he looks more confused than angry. I'm sure I can talk him around. I always could with his dad. "Look what she's done to my throat Shaun." I pull my neckline down.

"If you can stay with a woman like that, then God help you. She's never wanted me here. You know that yourself."

"And now I know why. She's on police bail for God's sake – all because of you. Why are you trying to ruin her life? All our lives." Oh God. The anger is starting.

"You've changed your tune – it's..."

"It's nothing to do with changing my tune. You could have, and might still get her a criminal record. You'll have to retract your statement Mum."

"Absolutely not a chance." My voice echoes around the en-suite. What a place for an argument.

"Where's a criminal record going to leave her?"

"It's not like she's ever had a proper job, is it?" I hiss at him. "Not with you bankrolling her, not to mention her mummy and daddy."

"Mum! It's got nothing to do with you how we live our lives." He stands from the shower seat, towering over me.

"It's got *everything* to do with me. When I see the example she's setting my grandchildren..."

"I'm going to have to put this right." He steps towards me with a look on his face I've never seen before. It's as though he hates me. He used to follow me around the house when he was little. We used to be each other's world. He used to...

"Get out of my way Mum."

"Don't you dare speak to me like that. Where do you think you're going anyway?" I step backwards, into the bedroom.

"To bring Danielle home from her mum's. I'm going to sort this mess out, once and for all."

"What about me? What's going to happen to me? I'm still getting over a stroke." I can't believe he overheard my phone call. He was as quiet as a corpse in the en-suite. What a fool I've been.

"That's really all you care about, isn't it Mum? What's going to happen to *you*." He swings around and faces me in the bedroom.

"No, I care about you. The kids. Danielle has never been good enough..."

"Let me past Mum. And I'd get packing if I were you. You can't stay here after this. As soon as I get back, I'm taking you home."

"Not until you listen to me. You're better off without her – you know you are. Now Leanne. She's..."

"I want nothing more to do with you Mum. Nothing. And if you don't retract your statement, you won't be seeing the children again either."

He storms past me, knocking me off kilter. Luckily, I land on the bed. He doesn't even look back to check if I am alright. Instead, he thumps down the stairs and then I hear the front door bang.

What have I done?

14

DANIELLE

MUM TRIED TO STOP ME, but I've got to put things right. Which is why I'm now heading, in Dad's Audi, back home. I know I'm on bail and there's a possibility they might just get me locked up again, but it's worth the risk.

I've got to get Jeannie to own up. I'm sure there's an element of nicety in her somewhere. She loves her son, after all. She also loves her grandchildren. We're both mothers when all's said and done. I *have* to get through to her? Call some sort of truce if need be.

I'm in terrible trouble for grabbing her yesterday and know I've got some making up to the children to do. But I can fix this. I've got to fix this. A red mist descended over me – what I did yesterday is not the way I would normally behave, and I'm genuinely sorry.

I can't have people think I've been systematically abusing my mother-in-law. I tried to speak to Leanne earlier, but she said she'd been advised not to communicate with me. Professionally or personally. That really hurt. Jeannie's got her well and truly suckered in. But then, she's always been able to talk the talk. A seventy-two-year-old woman, recovering from a stroke, covered in alleged grab and poke marks. No, I cannot blame Leanne really. The only way forward is to speak to Jeannie now. Level with her. See if we can all find a way forward that involves her owning up. That's if they let me inside the house.

I park around the corner and gingerly head up the street. I don't want to announce my arrival by pulling the car up outside. I plan to sneak up the side of the wall, towards the porch, before I can be locked out. Everything looks so normal in our lovely suburban street, except it's far from normal.

"Is everything alright Danielle?"

I jump. I'm so focused on getting back home, and being let in, that I'm in a world of my own. I should have made sure no one was around before I started walking towards the house. I'm sure Pauline was in her garden yesterday, watching as they led me to the police car. By the curious way she is looking at me, I expect she'll want to know what is going on.

"Erm. Yes. Thanks for asking."

She takes a couple of steps towards me as though she's expecting me to talk about things.

"I'm in a rush Pauline. I'm sorry. I'll catch up with you another time."

"Oh. OK then. So long as you're alright."

I try to smile, but my gaze is set firmly on my driveway. My car is not there. Shaun must have gone out in it. Which is probably just as well. At least I can speak to Jeannie on her own, without Shaun stopping me from getting in. As I approach the door, I realise that I didn't pick up my keys when I was taken away yesterday. Damn! The front door's locked. I ring the doorbell. Nothing. After a few moments, I step back, away from the porch, to catch Jeannie peering around the lounge curtain.

"Let me in," I mouth at her, pointing back at the front door. She lets the curtain drop and I return to the door, expecting her to open it. But she doesn't. After a few moments, I call through the letterbox. "Jeannie. Open the door, please. I haven't got my key."

Nothing.

"Jeannie. I'm not here to cause trouble. I just want to talk."

Nothing.

"Come on Jeannie. Surely we can sort this out. We both love Shaun. We both love the children. Please Jeannie." I cannot believe what I've been reduced to. But I have a hell of a lot to lose.

I step back again, wondering what to do next, and notice Pauline watching me. And a neighbour in another garden. God, I'm obviously public enemy number one. I walk around the back. The last time I stood here was yesterday, as Shaun was kicking me out of my own home. It feels like a long time ago.

To my surprise I find the conservatory door is still unlocked. We live in such a quiet, low-crime area that it's not necessary to be hugely vigilant. This took Shaun some getting used to after growing up in an inner-city area. It's no wonder his mother wants to trade her flat for a new life around here. It's totally different to what she's been used to.

As I make my way through the kitchen and past the dining room, I notice the breakfast pots from the children haven't been cleared. I missed them so much this morning – I'm not used to waking up without their chatter and their mess. The house is in silence, which is both strange and unnerving.

My hand hovers over the handle of the lounge door for what feels like ages, as I gather enough courage to face Jeannie. I take a deep breath before entering the room, expecting to find her in the same place as yesterday, but hopefully, less hostile without an audience to play to. I knew she was devious and has always disliked me, but never imagined she would stoop as low as she has for the last couple of weeks. It's almost as though she had it all planned out. Nothing would surprise me. Yesterday caught me off guard and I'm ashamed for losing it.

But today, I'm calm, and definitely grateful that it's just me and her – no Shaun. I just want to talk to her. *But where is she?* She was looking out of the window a few minutes ago and I can sense her here somewhere. She's one of the few people I've known whose presence I can actually *feel*, and it's not a nice feeling.

"Jeannie?" I plant my foot on the bottom stair and slowly ascend the rest. I can't hear anything coming from her room. The quiet is eerie. Perhaps she's in the en-suite. Maybe she's trying to make out she's scared of me by hiding. Stupid woman. Both she and I know who the scary one is between us. The door drags on the thick pile of the carpet. She's not in here. I feel the usual irritation to see her clothes hung in the wardrobe and her belongings unpacked and in place all around the room. I am annoyed to see the wedding photo of Shaun and I has been removed from the dressing table. She's probably smashed it.

She clearly has no intention of going anywhere. I'm certain it was her plan to get me out all along. Surely the hospital would know if she'd faked her so-called stroke though. She's certainly milked the situation for all it is worth.

I wander from room to room. A sadness tugs at my belly as I look in mine and Shaun's room – and notice the bed having only been slept in on one side, Shaun's clothes are in a mound on the floor. I'm always going on at him for that. The curtains are still drawn too. There's a whiff of the aftershave I bought for his birthday in our en-suite which makes me miss him even more.

Tears fill my eyes as I close the door and look in the children's rooms one by one. Gemima's is always tidy. She takes after me. Her bed is made, her curtains have been opened. Everything is in its place. Benedict's is the complete opposite. We call his floor *the floordrobe*, as that's where all his clothes end up. I miss the children so much. I realise it's nearly home time, so no doubt Shaun will be bringing them back from school any time soon. I need to have spoken to Jeannie before they all get back.

How dare my mother-in-law come between me and my children? I can't even collect them myself because of the lies she's told. I check the children's playroom, well I call it that, they call it the TV games room, then the family bathroom. Where on earth is she? "Jeannie?" I call again into the silence, freezing as I hear a noise coming from somewhere on the ground floor.

The front door is ajar as I tiptoe back downstairs, which is strange. It was locked before, but now a bunch of what looks like Shaun's keys swing from the keyhole. I imagine she's out in the street, raising the alarm against me. *My daughter-in-law is on bail to stay away. She's going to attack me. Please call the police!* Rage bubbles in my chest. I can't believe how much the woman has lied about me. I should have fought harder against Shaun. For the children's sakes as much as mine. That woman should *never* have come to stay in our home. I suspected what she was capable of, even if my short-sighted husband couldn't see it. I pull the door open. There's no sign of her out there. Thank God for that. There are enough people thinking bad things about me as it is.

My boots clip against the tiled floor as I head to the kitchen. Normally, it would be wonderful to be home after a night away. One of the best things about going away is returning. Home is my sanctuary – my favourite place in the world. I've spent many years making soft furnishings, cushions, rugs and curtains, to make it homely. And buying things such as paintings and one-off pieces of furniture. This is the home of my dreams and though it sounds like a cliché, we used to be a happy family. I could keep Jeannie at arm's length. I accepted her dislike of me and to keep the peace, I kept my distance. I would encourage Shaun to visit her on his own, sometimes taking the children. She's their grandmother, after all, and until recently, I would never have come between them. Even though it upset me when I found out she'd been bad-mouthing me in front of not just Shaun, but the children too.

I stiffen as I hear something clatter to the floor. The sound comes from Shaun's office. She must be in there. *Why?* I listen for a moment. The house lapses back into silence. The door creaks as I push it open.

She's standing behind Shaun's desk. My eyes meet hers, then fall on the shotgun on the desk in front of her. We stand there for what feels like a minute or two, as my heart rate increases. I locked the gun away myself, after Shaun went shooting the other day. I'm not technically supposed to know where the key is kept but Shaun was rushing out, late for an appointment. Yet for a second, I doubt myself. *Did I definitely lock the cabinet?* Maybe he's had it back out, or Jeannie has found the key's hiding place and helped herself.

"What the hell are you doing?" The door of the office closes behind me. To look at her, nobody would believe she's ill in any shape or form. She'll never admit to fabricating the effects of her stroke just to get herself in here. She's never made any secret of her envy about this house of ours, and how much she'd like to be free of the flat she lives in. I know she regrets letting her own house go, but after Bob died, she said herself, she was rattling around inside it.

Lines of light from the blind stripe her face. "I could ask you the same question." Her voice is thick with hatred. "You're not supposed to be here. You're on bail Danielle. You're not supposed to be within spitting distance of this house."

I swallow. I have to stay calm. No way is she going to rile me again. She's not worth it. "I'm here to speak to you Jeannie," I begin. "To sort this situation out like two grown women."

Though, looking at the sneer her face is twisted into, I'm going to have next to no chance.

She doesn't answer and continues to stare at me, the sneer firmly spread across her face, which is very unnerving. What's even more unnerving is Shaun's gun on the desk in front of her. I guess she'd have to shoot me at close range to be sure to hit me though with her so-called weak arm. That's if she even knows what to do with a gun. I'll stay here, at the other side of the room from her. I'm not taking any chances. And I'm not taking my eyes off that gun. For the first time since she arrived from the hospital, she's fully dressed, right down to her polished shoes. She's even got gloves on.

"We both love Shaun," I continue. "We both love Gemima and Benedict. There has to be a way through this Jeannie. One where we can both save face."

Still, she says nothing. Her sneer has become an expression of defiance. "Look Jeannie, I take full responsibility for what happened yesterday. If you could only own up to the things you've said that aren't true about me..."

"No chance." She literally spits the words back at me.

I'm going to have to make her.

15

JEANNIE

"Why Jeannie? Why are you doing this to me?"

The wobble in Danielle's voice makes me despise her even more. It's so false.

"You never wanted me here. Right from the moment I arrived." She's obviously not aware that Shaun has set off to see her.

"Surely, you must be able to see why I didn't want you here, Jeannie?" She half laughs. "Look at how you've carried on since you arrived."

Danielle is nothing but a pampered princess. She's never wanted for anything. Not like me. I've spent my whole life scrabbling around, making ends meet. And before long my life over. The stroke I have just had has shown me that. And what have I ever amounted to? "All you've ever done is try to come between Shaun and me. And my grandchildren."

"That's not true. I've always encouraged them to visit you."

"Liar," I shout, the venom in my voice shocking me.

"I'd love for things to be different." Her voice is calm. "But you've *never* liked me Jeannie, not from the moment we met.

91

Just because I'm not bloody Simone. I never can be Simone. You haven't even tried to get to know me. Come on Jeannie. It's not too late."

"I can't believe how Shaun treated poor Simone. Carrying on with *you* behind her back."

"I didn't know he was engaged to her. It wasn't my fault. The only person you can blame is Shaun. Anyway, that's all ancient history now."

"Well, I'm still in touch with her." I smile at Danielle. "We're great friends, actually." She looks rough. For once she isn't wearing a speck of make-up and looks as though she's borrowed leggings and a jumper from her mother. I'd go as far as to say she looks frumpy. "You can't hold a candle to Simone."

"I'm not trying to hold a candle to anyone. I never have. I'm me."

"She was like a daughter to me." Danielle needs to know the severity of what she did. That it's not right to go around breaking couples up who are engaged. I remember when Bob had an affair. It was the most agonising thing I've ever been through and was probably why I had so much sympathy for Simone.

"I could've been like a daughter to you Jeannie. You've made things as they are."

"I wouldn't have wanted you to be like a daughter to me. You're nothing but a spoilt little witch. With your posh parents and a rich husband to sponge off. Me, I've had to come up the hard way."

"So you're jealous of me? That's ridiculous."

"What. Of *you.* Not in your current predicament Danielle. You'll be going to prison if I have anything to do with it. Your friend Leanne believes me. So do the police, and a court will too."

"So you're going to keep this up then? You've no intention of telling the truth?"

"About what?" I roll my glove down and rub at my wrist, perhaps inadvertently, to wind her up. I'm sweating under these gloves but can't risk leaving my prints on this gun. She obviously has no idea that Shaun has discovered the truth.

"About what? I could end up with a criminal record if you don't retract your false accusations. You might not like me, but surely the fact that I'm the mother of your grandchildren must count for something?" Her eyes don't leave the gun as she pleads with me. Shaun's been gone ages. This needs finishing before he gets back.

"I haven't come this far to retract any accusations Danielle."

"I could lose everything because of you." Her eyes narrow now. I think she's accepted she'll get nowhere with me. "Are you even poorly or have you fabricated that as well? I wouldn't put anything past you."

Nasty Danielle is back. I'm glad. It makes what I'm about to do easier.

I'd better get on with it. I'm stalling. It's no wonder really. At least this way, I can leave Shaun the greatest gift he'll ever have. Freedom. Release. The chance to pursue life with someone who deserves him.

He's going to send me home anyway. And after the conversation he overheard me having with Margaret, my reputation is in tatters. I'll be lucky if they ever let me see Gem-Gem and Benny again, after what has gone on between us all. I was home and dry. *Why did Shaun have to overhear my conversation?* It's ruined everything.

I look down at the gun on the polished desk, then jerk my head towards Danielle who's edged closer. Strangely, I'm more alert and energetic than I have been all week, especially after feeling so old, tired and depressed. Still, I've made this decision now and I *have* to follow it through no matter how scared I'm feeling. It's the only way I can absolutely ensure Danielle gets what she is due. I've lived most of my life and she's ruined what I might have had left of it. When she gets nearer, I'll…

"How did you get hold of that?" She nods towards Shaun's shotgun. There's a look on her face that says she's now wary of me. Good.

"Shaun shouldn't leave his keys lying around."

"It needs to go back. *You* need to go back." She points at the shotgun, then points at me.

"Go back, *where* exactly?"

"Back home. Leave us in peace. If you don't tell the truth. I'll see you in court. I've got people who'll speak up for me." Her mouth is set in a hard, straight line. "One of us has to go Jeannie."

"This is my family too. You've tried to come between us for long enough. The only way I'm leaving this house is in a box."

"That can be arranged." She takes another step towards the desk, her eyes not leaving the gun. Is she planning to…?

I reach out and snatch it up. "Come one step closer and I'll shoot you."

"Don't be so daft!" I can see by her face she doesn't think I'm capable. "Even *you* must be able to see that I'm not worth doing time for."

I raise the gun in the air and point it towards her. It's years since I've held a gun and I feel calm about it, considering. This is it. This is where it all ends. This is what everything has been geared towards.

"Jeannie. Give me the gun. Now." Danielle holds her arms out, surely knowing she cannot get through to me. I have no fear. I am going to do this. Then she lunges around the side of the desk.

I step back, away from her. I point the gun to the roof of my mouth, my weaker hand on the trigger. I takes every bit of strength I have to keep hold of it.

"Oh yeah!" She actually laughs. "So you're going to blow your own brains out. Excellent. Be my guest."

I lower the gun for a moment. "As long as they think *you've* done it. I've got nothing else to lose." The last thing I see is her eyes widen and her face fall as she dives towards me.

16

SHAUN

Even though they've been released, my wrists still feel raw from the handcuffs. At least they've accepted I wasn't involved in any way. I can go to Benedict and Gemima now. I wander along the hallway in a daze. The armed officer follows me towards the lounge. I have to keep it together and stay strong for the children. I'll hear the echo of that shot for as long as I live. I pause as I rest my hand on the lounge door handle. Our lives have changed forever.

Reality starts to drive over me. *How have I let this happen? And how could my wife, the absolute love of my life, have turned into a cold-bloodied murderer, capable of shooting her children's grandmother dead?"*

Two paramedics tap on the open door and call *hello* into the hallway.

"Come in." I'm taken aback by how ordinary my voice sounds, considering. Yet I feel like I can't breathe. I gesture towards my office. "They're all in there."

"Are we OK to come in?" The paramedic addresses the officer, ignoring me completely.

"It's safe," he replies. "Go on through."

After they've passed us, I look around at the officer. "I can't go in. How can I face the children after what they've just seen..." I'm shaking from head to toe.

"Did they see it happen?"

"No. All of us just saw the immediate aftermath, which was bad enough. We heard the bang as we pulled up on the driveway. I can't believe my mother is dead. I can't believe that Danielle would be capable of such a thing." I know I'm wittering away to a complete stranger here.

"You'll get the chance to tell your side of things soon. Is there anyone who'll take the children whilst we interview you?"

"I don't know. I can't think straight right now. I'll sort something out – I just need to make sure they're OK."

It feels as though time has gone into slow motion as I push the lounge door open. As though nothing is real. When I walk into the room, the children are clinging to each other." *How are they ever going to get over this?* I don't see how counselling could even scratch the surface.

"I'm here," I say, enveloping them both in my arms, needing their closeness. Our lives will never be the same.

"I want Mum," sobs Benedict. "And Grandma."

"I know. So do I." The children's faces are as ashen as Mum's was. What I saw in that office is a vision that will never leave me. My mother shot dead on the floor, blood seeping from her head. My wife looking on, unable to speak, due no doubt to the enormity of what she's done. I look back towards the officer who stands in the doorway.

I've not just lost my mother. I've lost them both. Danielle will be sent to prison for years after what she has done. She could even get a life sentence. She's certainly left me and the children with one. What the hell are we going to do? We'll have to move. I can't stay here. Not now. Every time I walk into the house, I'll see it all over again. In fact, I need to get us out of here today. God knows where we'll go.

Footsteps and low voices travel up and down the hallway. The officer comes into the room and the door falls shut behind him. He stands next to the fireplace. More car doors bang and police radios beep and hiss. Voices and footsteps echo up and down the hallway.

"Are you alright staying with the children for a few minutes?" I relax my hold on them. "Whilst I see what's going on."

"I'm sorry you can't go out there."

Gemima grips onto my arm. "Don't go Daddy. Don't leave us." She hasn't called me daddy in years.

"I promise I'll be straight back." I shake myself free from her grasp as I hear footsteps in the hallway. "I need to find out what's happening."

As I open the lounge door, Danielle is being led, for the second time this week, towards our front door, by the police.

"How could you do this to our family?" I say as our eyes meet. "You've ruined so many lives, including your own."

"Come back in here Sir." The officer is behind me.

I ignore him. It's the only chance I'm going to get to speak to Danielle. Who knows when I'll see her again?"

"I didn't do it Shaun. I came back here to talk. Somehow there'll be evidence to prove I'm innocent of this." Her voice and eyes so gentle that she could almost be telling the truth. But she must have done it. No one else was here.

"Come on." One of the armed officers that was sent in to make the house safe, steers her closer to the door. "Let's get you to the car."

"I hope you rot after what you've done to my mother," I yell after her. "You're no wife of mine anymore."

"She shot herself." Danielle glances back over her shoulder.

"Just like the bruising. She's a liar and it will all come out. You'll see."

"I won't," I mutter, more to myself as she is led up the drive. "I'll never *see*. Ever."

17

DANIELLE

IT's four weeks to the day since I've seen my husband and children, and I pine for them more with each hour that passes. Part of my bail conditions are not to make contact, directly or indirectly, with any of them. I can't even telephone just to hear their voices.

Yesterday, Mum had to stop me driving to the school to get a glimpse of Shaun picking them up. "You get caught doing that and you'll be remanded until your trial. Is it really worth it Danielle?"

I knew what she was saying was right. Staying at my parents isn't ideal, but it's better than being locked up in some hellhole of a prison cell. At least they granted me bail when I was up in court the day after Jeannie died. The police wasted no time in charging me, even though my solicitor assured me the evidence was mainly circumstantial.

But thankfully, the magistrate could see that I didn't pose a danger to anyone. Surely, the jury will realise this as well. The only *danger* that has formed part of this situation has been Jeannie. She clearly would stop at nothing to get me out of the picture.

Which is why I personally ensured that the key to the gun cabinet had been labelled and left on her bedside table. I'd also ensured that the gun was fully loaded, though I'd obviously assured Shaun that I'd emptied it for him, after his clay pigeon shooting.

I knew Jeannie better than she knew herself and though I hadn't expected her to blow her own brains out; I knew she wouldn't be able to resist gaining access to it to further her cause in some way.

Really, I'd only expected her to threaten me with the gun, and that would have been more than enough to strengthen my case. It would have persuaded Shaun to send her back to her flat.

Just before our altercation, he'd turned up at Mum's, allegedly having found out about the lies Jeannie had been telling him, Leanne and the police. He'd come to pick me up and take me home. That makes the fact that he now believes me capable of shooting his mother dead, doubly hard to bear.

But today my resolve has weakened. I'm beyond desperate to see my children – even a glimpse. Just to know they're alright. I sit in the window of the public library, which faces the entrance to the school, pretending to bury my nose in a book, whilst regularly glancing across the road. I should be standing over there, waiting to have book bags and coats thrust at me. Waiting to hear all about their day.

I spot them straight away. Benedict first, followed by Gemima. They look for each other and then appear to be looking for their dad. They should be looking for me. But they seem OK. Clean, well dressed, smiling, normal. Living without me. Tears burn at the back of my eyes.

Then I see him. My Shaun. My stomach twists and contracts as he lets go of a woman's hand and waves at our children. They run to him. The woman ruffles the top of

Benedict's head. Then she turns and I'm certain that she looks straight at me.

Shaun is with Leanne. It seems everything Jeannie set out to do came to fruition. I can't believe how she has come between me and my children – even in death.

Before you go...

Thanks so much for reading your free novella A Life for a Life - I really hope you enjoyed it and will consider leaving me a review as this makes such a difference in helping other readers find the book.

Join my 'keep in touch' list to receive another free book, and to be kept posted of special offers and new releases. You can also join by visiting my website https://www.mariafrankland. co.uk/

ABOUT THE AUTHOR

Q: **Where do your ideas come from?**

A: I'm no stranger to turbulent times, and these provide lots of raw material. People, places, situations, experiences – they're all great novel fodder!

Q: **Why do you write domestic thrillers?**

A: I'm intrigued why people can be most at risk from someone who should love them. Novels are a safe place to explore the worst of toxic relationships.

Q: **Does that mean you're a dark person?**

A: We thriller writers pour our darkness into stories, so we're the nicest people you could meet – it's those romance writers you should watch...

Q: **What do readers say?**

A: That I write gripping stories with unexpected twists, about people you could know and situations that could happen to anyone. So beware...

Q: **What's the best thing about being a writer?**

A: You lovely readers. I read all my reviews, and answer all emails and social media comments. Hearing from readers absolutely makes my day, whether it's via email or through social media.

Q: Who are you and where are you from?

A: A born 'n' bred Yorkshire lass, with two grown up sons and a Sproodle called Molly. (Springer/Poodle!) The last decade has been the best so far: I've done an MA in Creative Writing, made writing my full time job, and found the happy-ever-after that doesn't exist in my writing - after marrying for the second time just before the pandemic.

Q: Do you have a newsletter I could join?

A: I certainly do. Go to https://www.mariafrankland.co.uk/ to join my awesome community of readers. I'll send you a free novella – 'The Brother in Law.'